Blueberries and Whipped Cream

Sylvia McNicoll

Cover by
Vlasta Van Kampen

gage EDUCATIONAL PUBLISHING COMPANY
A DIVISION OF CANADA PUBLISHING CORPORATION
TORONTO ONTARIO CANADA

To big-hearted Al,
who is smiling somewhere in another room

Canadian Cataloguing in Publication Data
McNicoll, Sylvia, 1954-
  Blueberries and whipped cream

(Jeanpac paperback original)
ISBN 0-7715-7017-1

I. Van Kampen, Vlasta.   II. Title.   III. Series:
Jean pac paperback original.

PS8575.N52B58 1988   jC813'.54   C88-094071-9
PZ7.M265B1 1988

Design: Marc Mireault

ISBN: 0-7715-**7017-1**

  2 3 4 5 6 7 8 9 WC 96 95 94 93 92 91

Written, Printed, and Bound in Canada

CHAPTER 1

The intercom crackled on: *Would Christina Dzuba report to the office, please? Christina Dzuba.*

What now?

It had been a rotten morning already. First, I slept in. Then I had to scramble for clean clothes out of the dryer and dash off to school without eating any breakfast. It seemed like I'd never get used to Mom being in the hospital.

By eleven o'clock math class my stomach sounded like a bowling alley. Everyone around me was snickering—except Mark, who didn't pay any attention at all at first.

He was too busy staring at Candy Thompson. She was wearing a tight, red sweater. A very tight, red sweater. When she saw Mark looking her way, she focussed her brown, Bambi eyes on him and smirked that silly smile of hers. You'd think she could leave just one guy in the school alone! It was enough to make me gag.

Then the bowling alley got louder. Besides groaning and rumbling, my stomach started squeaking occasionally. I shifted around in my chair, crossed my legs, and pretended not to notice the noise.

It didn't work. Mark turned around. "Here," he said, tossing me a piece of gum. "This'll tide you over to lunch."

1

Now, this wasn't the kind of attention I wanted from him. He had these great, green eyes and when he looked at me, I mean really looked at me, with no Candy to distract him, I went weak.

"Thanks," I answered. What else could I say? Then he smiled in a smooth, sexy kind of way, a way that said, "Don't worry. You're special, Christina."

But it was just then that things really began to go wrong.

When the intercom crackled out my name, Mark looked at me, one eyebrow raised in question. I shrugged my shoulders. The last time they wanted me in the office was because Old Cedar Chest, my history teacher, had accidentally marked me absent. Easy to do, since I have zero to say in his class. Had he done it again? I wasn't too worried as I left the room and headed for the stairs.

But outside the office, I found Pop waiting for me, and alarms went off in my head. What's he doing here, I thought.

There he stood—short and round, with his beer belly hanging over his belt. He looked like some kind of miniature Santa Claus. He was wearing his hard hat like he always does, plus dirty old work clothes and steel-toed boots, and carrying—geez, how embarrassing—his big, black lunch pail.

"Christa, hi. You'll have lunch with me?"

That name—I hate it when he calls me that, it's so Slovak. I was so embarrassed I forgot about being worried. All I wanted was to get out quickly before the bell rang and my friends, maybe even Mark, noticed

2

us. "Sure, Pop," I mumbled as I headed toward the door.

He drove me to a park on the outskirts of town. The kids from school never went there, which was fine by me. No one would see us. We found a bench and sat down.

Pop opened his black box and took out his thermos and some kaiser buns filled with mock chicken. He poured me a cup of tea, complete with lemon and sugar, the way I like it. But then it hit me—he doesn't drink his tea this way. He made this lunch especially for me. That's why he came to school.

"Hey, Pop, how'd you know I forgot my lunch?" I asked him.

"You forgot your lunch? Yeah, well, I came back from the hospital to pick up something of Mama's. Just thought we'd talk and have a nice lunch together."

It was a decent thing for him to do. I knew I should be grateful. But why couldn't he take me out for a burger like a normal parent? Why did he take me to the park like I'm still a six-year-old who loves to picnic?

You can't do this, Pop, I wanted to say. *You can't just pick up where we left off. I'm not six years old any more.*

Then I noticed he was throwing bread crusts to the pigeons. Something else we used to do when I was little. Somehow I felt like doing it again now, too. I had almost finished my roll and started breaking off pieces.

"Eat the other one too," Pop said without looking up from the pigeons. "I made both for you. You're too skinny."

I sipped some tea and polished off the second roll.

Then I looked at my father as he stared straight ahead at the birds. The skin around his eyes was all scrunched up as though he were smiling—or maybe wincing. There was an odd look on his face.

A sick, scared feeling came over me. "She's not coming home any more is she, Pop." I didn't even say it as a question.

He shook his head.

One part of me, the mature fifteen-year-old, should have expected this. Her surgery had been unsuccessful, the chemotherapy hadn't worked. She'd lost all her hair and a lot of weight from the radiation treatment. She didn't even look like my mom any more. So why hadn't I pieced it all together?

Because there was still this six-year-old inside me, ripping up crusts and flinging them at the birds like it was all their fault. The six-year-old wished on stars, threw pennies in fountains, lit candles in churches, and prayed and prayed for God to make her mom better. And it was that six-year-old, sitting beside Pop on the park bench, who started blubbering as though she'd never stop.

"Ah, Christa," was all Pop could say. He was sighing and shaking his head. "Ah, Christa," he repeated and patted my back.

There was nothing he could do to calm me down. I

4

was hiccup-crying now and I could taste some of my sandwich coming back on me.

Then I threw up.

Pop took his handkerchief and dipped it in the drinking fountain. He handed it to me. I wiped my face, rinsed the handkerchief out in the fountain and took a long drink. I gave the handkerchief back to Pop.

"Have you told Ron already?" I said when I could speak.

"He went with me when I talked to Dr. Worden."

"Why didn't you take me?"

"Ronnie's the oldest. He's almost a man."

"C'mon, Pop," I said weakly. Any other time, I would have given him an argument.

"Christa, you would have cried and then we all would have bawled. What good would that have done?"

I thought—she's my mother, I had the right to be there, too. I wanted to be there. But there was no point in saying that now. It wasn't worth the effort. I just nodded in silence.

Pop hesitated for a moment and then he took out of his pocket what looked like a crumpled old tissue. He unfolded it and removed something from it. "Here. Mama wants you to have this." He placed her wedding band in my hand and closed my fingers over it. "It keeps falling off her finger."

I started hiccupping again.

"You want to come and see her now?" My father said when I settled down a bit.

5

"No, Pop. I can't."

"There's not too much time left, Christa. We won't know from one moment to the next—"

"No!" I shouted. I shouldn't have yelled at him but I felt angry all of a sudden.

"She tried so hard to fight this...everything they told her might work, she went through with, no matter how sick it made her." He threw up his hands. Was he angry at me? "You want me to drop you back off at school or what?"

"No, I'll just sit here awhile."

"O.K.," he said. His shoulders slumped.

Fine, you're disappointed in *me* for a change, I thought.

He walked away without looking back.

Long minutes passed. Finally, I opened the fist that was clutching Mom's ring. For the first time I looked at it close up, turning it over. Inside the wide yellow band were her initials—S.M. for Sonja Mahovalich— and my father's—P.D. for Paul Dzuba. I don't think my mother had ever taken that ring off before. The fact that it was in my hand now meant she had really given up.

"I don't want your stupid ring," I said out loud. *I want my mommy*, screamed the six-year-old inside. Then I slipped the ring on my finger.

CHAPTER 2

Mom always believed in starting the day with a hot breakfast. When we were younger, Ron and I must have been the only kids on the block to have our cornflakes served with hot milk. Not only did she make our breakfast, but up until she went into the hospital, she got us up early to make sure we ate it as well.

Ron hated that. Sleeping in was important to him. His temper was at its worst in the mornings and he would swear at Mom as she tried, for maybe the eighth time, to get him to the breakfast table.

Things were different now. The day after finding out Mom was going to die, I got up and Ron was already at the kitchen table. As I moved around, I felt like I'd been split in two. One half of me was a machine. The machine made toast, packed a lunch, and cleared the breakfast dishes off the table. The other half—the human one—stood back numbly and watched.

Ron's eyes, I noticed, couldn't meet mine. That was O.K. I knew that if we really looked at each other, right in the eyes, we'd see something there that would penetrate the comforting numbness. We'd have to acknowledge that, yes, Mom was dying.

"Ron, there's ice cream in this bowl," I said, breaking the unspoken pact. I'd just noticed that the small white pool in his bowl was too lumpy to be milk.

He didn't answer.

"Ron, you're not having ice cream for breakfast—are you?" It suddenly became very important that he answer me.

"Shut up, it's none of your business," he snapped. He stalked out of the kitchen, went into his room, and slammed the door. The house became very quiet.

After a moment, I heard a sound—like a tearing noise—coming from Ron's room, and then Ron's voice, muffled, calling, "Mom, Mom."

I ran into his room. Ron was sprawled on his bed, face in his arms, sobbing. His jeans had split up the back.

Another time I would have laughed. "I'll fix them. I can use Mom's machine," I pleaded with him. "It's O.K., really it is."

"Just leave me alone," he said through clenched teeth. His voice was so full of anger, it shocked me. He turned over and his eyes looked into mine. I saw in them the pain and helplessness that I felt too. My heart ached right into my throat.

I turned and left the room. I wanted to cry. We should be leaning on each other, I thought. Instead, Ron was acting as though he hated me.

Though we went to the same school, Ron rushed out ahead of me. The Detention King was going to arrive at school early for once.

As I watched him go, I wanted to yell after him,

"What did I *do*?" I shrugged, collected up his jeans from his bedroom floor, went into my parents' room, and switched on Mom's sewing machine.

It was an ugly old black thing that Mom had salvaged from Electro-Knit's rejects. That's where she used to work before she got sick. I guided the jeans under the needle. Mom's wedding band clicked against the throat plate.

I squeezed my eyes tightly against the sadness.

Other feelings were churning around inside me, too. Like anger. I mean, here I was sewing Ron's pants after taking his verbal abuse. Just like Mom. Was I taking over for her? Was that what this ring was about?

It isn't fair, I thought furiously. I won't do it!

But I finished the jeans and draped them over a chair in Ron's room. Then I went into my room, yanked off the ring, and threw it in my jewellery box.

I collected up my things and left for school.

Jennifer, my best friend, was already at the lockers when I got there. She was standing on her toes re-arranging things on the top shelf. Her locker was right next to mine.

"Hi, Chris, how's it going?" she said without looking away from the shelf.

I didn't answer. She didn't seem to notice. I was trying my locker combination for the third time. No good that time, either.

"Hey, where'd you go yesterday? Mark was looking for you." She glanced sideways at me.

I slammed my fist on the locker, then turned away and covered my face with my hand.

Jennifer finally stopped rearranging. She watched me for a few seconds, then reached over. "Here," she said softly, "let me." She manoeuvred the lock around and back and tugged it open.

"Thanks," I mumbled.

She waited a few moments for me to say something more. I didn't.

"Is it your mom?" she asked finally.

I nodded. Stop looking at me, I thought, or I'll cry. "I can't talk about it," I added quickly.

Jennifer chewed on the inside of her cheeks. "O.K.," she floundered. "Sorry." Her voice was barely a whisper. I could tell that she understood. Then she touched my shoulder gently and it was all I could do not to break down.

How was I going to get through this day? How was I going to get through the rest of my life?

CHAPTER 3

Mrs. Chang's voice droned on. Home economics class. I wasn't paying much attention. There were so many thoughts I had to turn off that I found I couldn't focus on the moment-to-moment ordinary things either.

What was she talking about?

"Buy the fabric, paying close attention to the instructions on the back of the pattern envelope." Oh, our new sewing project. Mrs. Chang flipped over her sample pattern and pointed out where to look for various pieces of information. Already the blackboard was full of her notes—written in tiny, neat writing that resembled her hand stitching. Mom would have loved her.

I don't know why that made me so angry.

I hated home economics. It was too much like introductory housewifery for me. What I'd really wanted to take was technical drawing, but Mom and Pop wouldn't let me. I would've loved to draw blueprints on those slanted tables in the technical drawing classroom. Instead, I was stuck in another kitchen—this one with a lot of sewing machines in it.

"Now, girls, I want you to find a partner and measure each other to determine your correct size. Three measurements. . . ." She held up three fingers.

Then she took a huge pattern book with a female silhouette on the back cover, and pointed again. "Bust, waist, and hips. And, girls"—she paused to make sure everyone was paying attention—"quietly, please."

I had to move quickly and find someone so as not to call attention to myself.

There was a lot of giggling. Mrs. Chang walked around the room as we were measuring. Closer and closer she drifted. Finally she stopped at my partner and me. She shifted the tape upwards to measure my bust line. She frowned. What was the matter? Couldn't she believe the number she was looking at?

Just leave me alone for once, I silently pleaded.

No luck.

"You know, Christina, you didn't enjoy sewing that apron last term. Why don't you pick something you really would like to make? Perhaps a frock for the school dance."

A frock? Nobody uses that word anymore. Besides, how could I sew a "frock" for the school dance? I doubted that I'd ever want to go to a dance again. But then I thought about Mark—his uneven grin, those green eyes that always invited me to melt into them. Imagine going to a dance with him! It would be like entering a whole new life, a new world. I caught myself smiling.

"I see the idea appeals to you. Good," Mrs. Chang continued. "Now, don't choose an elaborate designer pattern. Something simple that's well-sewn can be just as attractive."

I nodded. She moved on. Now I was stuck with having to make a "frock." It meant shopping for the pattern and material—things I didn't think I could face—and it meant doing it quickly because I was supposed to start working on it in class this week. Maybe Jennifer could go shopping with me at the mall after school. That would make it bearable.

Mom. I was supposed to visit her at the hospital today. It was the last thing in a million years that I wanted to do. When I wasn't sad about her dying, I was angry at her. It didn't make sense, but it felt like she was deserting me, leaving me all alone. When I wasn't missing her, I almost hated her.

Then Mark caught up with me in the hall between classes. "Hey, Legs," he called after me. At least he didn't call me Skinny or Stilts, the way the other guys did. "Slow down," he said, smiling. I love that smile. Despite everything, it turned a hundred-watt-bulb on inside me.

I stopped.

"Where'd you go yesterday, anyway?" He didn't notice that I wasn't answering. "There's a basketball practice after school today, did you hear?"

"No, Jennifer didn't tell me."

"Well then, will I see you after school?" Those eyes wouldn't let me alone. C'mon, c'mon, they kept saying. In our school, hanging around together for basketball practice was equal to going out, although we still weren't really an official couple yet. How could I turn him down?

"Sure," I said. *Yes, yes*, my insides screamed. I was

so happy—and relieved. I couldn't visit Mom today, I just couldn't. I knew she'd understand.

But I also knew I should go to the hospital. I didn't want to, but I knew I should. I'll feel bad about it later if I don't go, I said to myself. I'll visit her tomorrow, I promised, and tried to put Mom out of my mind.

Not an easy thing to do. Mostly, I *did* think about her, and the nightmare stayed with me. Even when I didn't, something kept gnawing at my insides.

By the last class of the day, math, I was still all mixed up. I felt so bad I just wanted to do something to make me feel good. I doodled on my loose-leaf paper.

Mr. MacDonald had a sixth sense for anyone who was daydreaming. "Christina," he called. "Would you work out this problem on the board, please?"

I hate doing things on the board. Everyone watches me, and I feel like a Douglas fir, being so tall and thin. Today I hadn't even attempted to listen or work out the example. I was going to look like a complete idiot.

While I hesitated, Mark slipped something onto my desk. It was his working-out of the problem. I mouthed a quick thank you to him. He winked and smiled. I felt myself lighting up again.

Then I walked to the board.

Mark's numbers were a bit hard to make out, but it was still a lot easier than if I'd had to do the problem from scratch.

Mr. MacDonald nodded when I was finished, and then I thought I was hearing things. "Thank you, Mark," he said.

I guess I turned red, but Mr. MacDonald winked at me the same way Mark had. "Confine your thoughts to math, Miss Dzuba, during this period, if you please." He said it as though he knew what I was thinking and he sort of looked at Mark as though it was him I was thinking about.

The class laughed, but I didn't mind. Nobody knew what was really on my mind. I'd rather be laughed at than pitied. Besides, Mr. MacDonald had linked Mark and me together publicly, which was O.K. by me. Maybe that would scare Candy away.

After school, I walked to the gym with Mark. He was very tall and I didn't feel like a Douglas fir beside him.

"Don't worry about Big Mac, he's coaching our team this year and he's great."

"Yeah?" I needed to pinch myself I felt so good.

He walked ahead so that he could push open the gym door for me. Then he put his hand on my lower back and guided me through. None of the other guys did this kind of thing. But that was what I liked about Mark. He wasn't like the other guys.

Some of his friends were already there, dribbling and shooting baskets. One of them whistled. So juvenile—but I couldn't help smiling.

Mark ignored him. We stopped before going into the separate locker rooms. He grabbed my hand and held it for a few seconds, looking straight into my eyes. "See you later," he said like he was saying much, much more. I had to pull my hand away finally, so I could go and change.

When I was all ready, I rushed out to the smaller gym where the girls were practising.

You can't imagine how great it felt to dribble the ball, shoot it, and hear it swoosh through the basket. It was something in my life I had control over.

We practised lay ups, passing, and shooting. After that we had a scrimmage. Through it all I never had time to stop and think—hey, my mother is dying.

But she was and I should have been visiting her.

There was still time to go to the hospital after the practice was over, but I stayed to play a game of twenty-one with Mark. My shots were all on target. So were his. It ended up a tie. Mark laughed and shook my hand. But then he didn't let go. And there we were holding hands.

"Get out of here. Go do your math homework," Big Mac yelled as he came out of his office.

"Sure, boss," Mark answered with a mock salute. I think he would have kissed me if Big Mac hadn't kept standing there with his hands on his hips. He was waiting for us to separate and go into our locker rooms. So we had to.

"Can I walk you home, Christina?" Mark was waiting for me outside the gym. It was one of the few times he'd used my real name.

Home, home.

"Uh, no...I promised I'd walk with Jen...." I couldn't tell him that I didn't want my brother or father to see me with him today.

"O.K.," he answered and then he left, looking puzzled.

I really did walk home with Jennifer. She wasn't talking. Was that on my account or was it because of the practice?

It didn't look like she was going to make the team this year, not even as a spare. She wasn't really tall enough and she wasn't quick about snatching the ball away from an opponent. Too many ballet lessons. I knew she was feeling low.

And suddenly I needed her to jabber away about just anything that was frivolous and happy. I didn't want all that dead air between us. I didn't want to be able to think. "Any guy on the team that you like this year?" I asked, hoping to start her off.

Jennifer looked puzzled, then she blushed and smiled.

"You dog! Who? Who?"

"Wayne," she answered.

"Wayne Dryden!" I was amazed. "How come you never told me?" As I said it, I knew the answer. When could she have? When I was crying about my mom, or rushing home to do the laundry, or walking to the gym with Mark? I hadn't been much of a best friend lately.

"Why don't you give cheerleading a whirl this year?" I suggested to Jennifer. "You'll get to be around the guys' team more—you know, on the team bus and that."

She twisted her mouth and frowned at me. "That would be sinking low, wouldn't it?" she said. "Pom-poms know more about basketball than Riverdale cheerleaders."

She was right and it was time for her to turn off my route home.

"You wanna come to the mall after school tomorrow? Only for about an hour, though. I have to visit my mother after."

"Sure," she said enthusiastically. I guess she did miss doing fun things together.

"O.K. See you."

"Bye." Jennifer called back.

Right. I have to visit my mother *after*, I repeated to myself. Now I had to face my father.

I walked in our front door and saw the wagon train of empty beer bottles on the coffee table.

"Hi, Pop," I said to him. He was working on another bottle.

"We missed you at the hospital."

"Yeah well, I meant to go but there was basketball practice after school and—"

"So what about after?"

"I thought I better come home and make supper for you and Ron," I lied quickly. I really wasn't sure why I couldn't face Mom today.

"We ate already—hamburgers—at the hospital with Mama."

"Oh well, I didn't know that," I said, totally peeved. Ron and my dad were always doing things together, sneaky-like, behind my back.

"Well, Mama thought she might be able to get a milkshake down, so we tried. She had a real good day today."

"Yeah?" So why all the beer, I wanted to add.

"Yeah, so that's why I wished you had showed your face," he said through his teeth. He looked like Ron when he did that.

"Me too, Pop," I said. You don't argue with my dad after seven beers—you avoid him. I learned that at an early age.

CHAPTER 4

I was about six years old when I learned about Pop's drinking.

He was working at Maple Grove Packers when the whole line got laid off because their beef jerky wasn't selling. Mom was expecting a baby at the time.

Being six years old, I didn't care. I thought it would be nice to have Pop home. The day it happened, he promised to take me fishing later in the week when Ron went to the circus with the Cubs. The next day, he went to the unemployment office to fill out some forms. He left right after lunch. Supper was usually early, but hours later we were still waiting. Had something happened to him? Had he been hit by a car? Finally, we started supper without him. We were eating without talking when Mom doubled over. She was breathing funny and looked white and sick.

"Get to bed," she gasped.

Ron and I went. I don't know how it happened, but next day Mom was in the hospital, and Pop was sprawled out on the couch.

That was the day we were supposed to go fishing. I got up early and dressed. Then I shook Pop roughly to wake him up.

"Stop it, stop it," he mumbled, brushing me off, still asleep.

I shook him harder. This was important. It was our day to be together. We had to dig for worms and everyone knew the fish bit best in the morning. Finally I got a glass of water and poured it over him.

Pop woke up.

He lashed out at me with the back of his hand and I was thrown hard against the wall. The blow knocked the breath out of me so that I couldn't even cry. Then, when I could breathe again, I refused to. I just stood and stared at him. He sputtered for a while and then stalked off.

I still hadn't fully grasped the ugliness of his mood. I went up to him later when he was having a cup of coffee at the table. Hairbrush and elastics in hand, I insisted he French braid my hair—the way Mommy did it.

Imagine asking him—with his thick calloused fingers—to French braid my hair! His hands must have been shaking from all the alcohol he had consumed the night before as well.

He yanked at my hair roughly and scraped my scalp with the brush's metal bristles.

I didn't understand. Why was he acting this way?

He cursed low under his breath as at last he wound the elastic around my hair. He thought he was finished.

"This won't hold," I said with the tone of a monarch. He had always treated me like a princess—how else would I talk? Then I shook my head to prove the point and the braid fell apart.

I turned around and saw Pop's face too late—his

21

mouth crumpled into a sneer, his eyes skinny with loathing.

"You stupid kid," he said at the same moment that his open hand cracked against my face.

This man was not Pop. He was a stranger.

I ran away and hid.

Later, when the stranger turned back into Pop again, he had to coax me from the bottom of the linen closet.

"Christa, come out, please." I cringed further into the corner. "Come, come, we have to dig for worms, no?" he continued.

I wouldn't answer.

Pop rustled a bag of Smarties. "Look what I have for us to eat in the boat."

Then I knew it was my Pop again. I crawled out. And we did go fishing.

Pop rowed us out to the middle of the lake, threw me the large bag of Smarties, and went to sleep. I hooked a worm and hung my string into the water. Then I arranged my Smarties into rows by colour, the way I always did. I savored each one, sucking them, closing my eyes and trying to guess the flavour. They really all tasted the same. There were no fish around. How could there be in the middle of the lake in the middle of the day? It was too hot, and I was getting sticky. I played with my string a bit, yanking it and dropping it, making the worm do a crazy little dance.

Quietly, the sky blackened. I looked at Pop's face. His mouth was open and he was making funny bear noises. I knew it was going to rain, but I couldn't trust that person slumped in front of me. Was it Pop in there or the stranger? Should I wake him or not?

The sky rumbled then and a white crooked stick of lightning cracked into the water.

Pop started. "Huh? Christa? Why didn't you wake me?" He began rowing hard, not waiting for an answer.

The waters welled up around us. Our tiny boat rocked.

Another jagged lightning stick struck down out of the sky.

I just watched Pop. The storm didn't scare me as much as that stranger inside of Pop's body.

Of course we made it to shore. Afterwards, I heard Pop telling the story about how rough the water was, and how fierce the storm was, and how I never cried—what a brave little sailor I was.

I also heard that I had lost a baby brother.

And funny—that night, when we went to visit Mom and I needed to see her so badly, I couldn't go. A security guard stopped us because I was too young. I sat with the receptionist while Pop and my brother went up to Mom.

Somehow that six-year-old mixed up all the bad things—the storm, not being allowed to see Mom, not having a new baby brother—all of it got confused and knotted into a ball that I laid at my father's feet.

I learned that the ugly stranger snuck out of a bottle during bad times. I knew to avoid Pop then. In fact, I found it easier to avoid him altogether.

So I didn't only lose a baby brother.

CHAPTER 5

The morning after I had stayed for basketball practice with Mark, my brother, Ron, got on my case. I had my history book propped up on my teapot, doing some last minute studying for a quiz. I hadn't been able to concentrate on schoolwork the night before. Also, I thought that if Ron continued to ignore me, it wouldn't matter so much if I was too occupied to notice.

I didn't see him standing in front of me. Ron came up and flicked my book over. Geez, I hate that.

So I took the tea bag out of the pot and poured myself a cup without saying anything.

"Where's my socks?" Ron asked me.

"I give up. On your feet?"

"You know what I mean. When did you do the laundry last?"

"Think it was the day before yesterday." Ron was bending over close to me, reaching for the cereal. When I squeezed some lemon into my tea, I managed to squirt him, too. Good! "Maybe you should wear some from under your bed, since they'll never see the washing machine from there."

"Ah, shut up!"

"You shut up! What's the matter—missing your

24

servant? Bet you don't tell Mom to shut up any more."

His face went white, and I wished I could pull the words back inside me.

"At least I miss her," he shot back. "You can't even get your butt over to the hospital. Rather hang around with Mark Hasting, eh?"

"I came home to make your supper! You and Dad never asked me to go with you!" I was yelling now. It was all too much like that time when I was so small and alone, and I wasn't allowed to see Mom.

"Look," I said calming down. "I have to buy something for a school project tonight and I'm going to see Mom after. If you want socks, you'll have to wash some or buy some."

He clicked his tongue against his teeth in disgust, then walked away. I clicked my tongue back—only louder.

It was a great start to the day—and it never got better.

Jennifer couldn't come shopping. She had forgotten she had a dentist appointment after school.

Then there was Old Cedar Chest's "quiz." The blackboard was already full of essay questions when I came into the room. Cedar Chest, dressed in his favourite rumpled suit, paced up and down the aisles as we madly scribbled the questions down.

"Remember, I want treaties and dates. Back up all your statements."

I hate when a teacher starts to talk at you before you've finished copying something off the board.

There—I was finished. Now to answer the questions. "In what way was the Second World War a repeat performance of the first?"

Hmm. I chewed my pencil. When I smelled Old Cedar Chest—he really did smell like he was trailing a cedar chest with him—I knew he was close. I had to write something down. "Germany lost again," I scribbled. Brilliant.

Why couldn't it be multiple choice? I'd have had some chance then. As it was, there was such a jumble of things in my head I couldn't sort out and catch hold of any history facts. The harder I tried, the blanker I went.

I debated whether to hand in an empty piece of paper. Maybe he'd think I was absent again or that he'd lost my test. I walked up to the front carrying a blank sheet of foolscap along with my quiz. I started to think I could do it, that I might get away with it. At the last moment, Old Cedar Chest looked at me over his black half-glasses. I was staring right into those watery blue eyes.

I handed in my one answer—*Germany lost again.*

The bell rang and it was midmorning break. I ran out before Cedar Chest had a chance to look at my test. And there was Mark in the hall.

He waved and I walked over to him. This time there was no other excuse—he took my hand just to hold it. The history test was fading from my mind fast.

"Hi, Legs. You going to shooting practice?"

"Yeah. You?"

"Sure. C'mon, we can practise together."

The coach had given us charts to fill in—how many baskets we made from different areas, that kind of thing. Mark showed me how to use my wrist more and it improved my score. Then we played one on one.

I was winning because he guarded me very loosely like he was afraid of hurting me. Then he changed his mind and played a lot tighter. I crashed into him.

"Foul on you." He quickly locked his arms around me. "I get two free shots." Then he pulled me in closer. "But isn't it worth it?"

His faced moved nearer to mine. His lips were maybe a couple of centimetres away from my mouth. But then the bell rang. I turned away quickly and his lips just brushed across my cheek.

That was definitely the only good fifteen minutes in my day.

In Mrs. Chang's class, we broiled grapefruit. Hoping we were going to cook something good, I hadn't bothered to pack a lunch. Imagine, all that playing around with a stupid piece of fruit! We had to cut it up, sprinkle it with brown sugar, "dot" it with butter, as Mrs. Chang would say, and stick it under the broiler. For the finishing touch, we topped it off with a cherry. Apart from the melted brown sugar mixed with the butter and the cherry, the grapefruit tasted every bit as disgusting as a grapefruit always tastes, only hotter.

I suddenly had a craving for one of Mom's cabbage rolls. Maybe I could ask her how to make them tonight and surprise everyone for supper.

By lunch time, I was starving, so Jennifer lent me some change to buy a soup in the cafeteria. We were in line together and as I swung around with my tray after paying, the day sunk to a new low.

I saw *them* together.

They were sitting close, chatting away. Candy's long red braid coiled invitingly down the middle of her back. I couldn't keep from staring at her. She touched Mark's arm as she laughed at some joke of his and I could have killed her.

I wanted him for me. I needed him now.

How could Mark do this to me?

"What a cow," Jennifer said when she saw where I was looking. "I overheard Wayne talking to Mark after French class. He said that Candy was a 'real woman' compared to the rest of us."

"She's awfully short for a 'real woman,'" I said knowing with a sick, green feeling that it didn't matter what I thought.

"Yeah, you'd think she'd topple over, wouldn't you?"

"Let's just change the subject, O.K.?" I kept my head down the rest of lunch, concentrating on my tasteless soup.

It was only as we were leaving the cafeteria that Mark noticed me.

"Coming to my game tonight?" he asked, as though nothing had happened.

"I can't, Mark," I said. I watched his eyes. They stopped looking at me as Candy walked by. She waved to him.

"Why not?" he asked.

"Because," I snapped. I might have told him about Mom, but he had just spent the lunch hour with Candy. Why should I explain anything to him?

His head jolted back as though I had slapped him. "Oh...O.K." I couldn't believe it, he looked genuinely upset. What did he expect of me? How could he have lunch with Candy and think he could just keep on with me?

"See you around," I said shortly.

Then I could've cried when he answered, "O.K., bye," and wandered off without me down the hall, taking those cool green eyes with him.

Why did everything have to be so complicated?

CHAPTER 6

I dragged myself to the mall after school. There was only one material store there, so I walked to it quickly without any window shopping or dawdling. I went over to the pattern tables, waited till someone finished with the Valencia catalogue and thumbed through the Sew-it-Easy section.

Whoops, I nearly missed it—Valencia 7684, a two-piece dress, no buttonholes, no zipper, no darts, and only four pattern pieces! Plus there was a V-shaped neckline that actually showed cleavage. It wasn't too plain either, the way Sew-it-Easy dresses usually are. There was something different about it under the neckline. The material twisted the way a shirt does when you tie it into a knot above your waist on a hot day. I wondered if that would be hard to do. Well, Mrs. Chang would be there to help.

I went over to the steel filing cabinet, pulled open a drawer, and fingered through the patterns, which were tightly wedged together—7682, 7683, 7684. Now size—size 8, oh-oh, no size 10, but phew, there it was, size 12. I had to pull with both hands to get it out.

Material next. I flipped over the envelope and checked under my size in the chart just the way Mrs. Chang had showed us. It needed two-and-a-half metres of cotton or wool jersey. I didn't care what

30

colour, but I didn't want to have to buy extra material to match stripes or checks or anything.

Jersey, jersey, jersey. I wandered around checking the bolts for the name of the material—I didn't know what jersey looked like—and for the price. Here was the bad news. When I found the right fabric, the price ranged from fifteen dollars to twenty dollars per metre. I couldn't even afford to sew the top.

But wait, Mom's old factory had an outlet that would be open now. I still had enough time to dash over there before it closed. I paid for the pattern and some straight pins that I also needed, then ran all eight blocks to the factory outlet.

The little bell over the door rang as I went in. I had to walk down a small flight of stairs.

"We're almost closing. Can I help you?" a pleasant voice asked me as I browsed. "Why, you're Sonja Dzuba's girl, aren't you?"

"Yes," I answered, hesitating.

"I'm Andrea Petrovitch. I met you at the Christmas Party a few years ago." I must have still looked puzzled. "Ah, but you don't recognize me. I was an elf. Now you remember?"

It must have been when I was about nine years old. But, oddly enough, I did recall her voice and smile, as though from another lifetime.

"How is your mom?"

"She's dying," I blurted out.

"Oh dear, oh dear!" she threw up her hands. "We liked her so much here at Electro-Knit. The girls will be so upset. I'm so sorry."

31

I was sorry too. I mean, that I had said it so bluntly and thrown her into such a panic. She seemed like a decent person.

She turned out to be better than decent. When she looked at my pattern, she dug out some material under the counter, black wool jersey and contrasting red, exactly the way the designer of the pattern had pictured it. She gave it to me for free. "Now if you ever need any other material for your sewing class, you come and see me." Her hand rested on my shoulder for a moment.

"Thank you, Mrs. Petrovitch."

"It's nothing. Electro-Knit worked poor Sonja so hard, it's the least they can do." She waved to me from the window as I ran down the street towards the hospital.

I was anxious to see my mother now. I was going to talk to her about Mrs. Petrovitch, the dress, and Mark, and ask her for the recipe for cabbage rolls. We would chat the way we used to do over the dishes. I really missed that. But when I got off the elevator at Mom's floor, it was a chamber of horrors.

At first it was quiet enough to hear the *sish* of a machine breathing for someone. My heels were making loud *click-click* noises that were bouncing off the walls so I tried tiptoeing, quickly. Then someone began chanting, loudly, as if in pain.

"Oh, please let me go.... Oh, please let me go."

There was a scurry of nurses to the room where the voice was coming from.

It continued for a few more minutes.

32

"Oh, please let me go. . . . Oh, please let me go."

Imagine, poor Mom was stuck in this place.

"Please, please, don't hurt meeee!" Whoever it was stopped abruptly.

I tried to talk myself out of the coldness that gripped at my insides. It doesn't matter, I'm going to see Mom. We're going to talk just like old times. About Mark, the dress, Mrs. Petrovitch.

But my enthusiasm was all gone. I sank back on my heels and walked slower and slower.

Then I was at the nursing station. There was no delaying it any more.

Nurse Frankson—that was the name on her little plastic badge, E. Frankson—put her finger to her lips as she guided me to Mom's room.

"Shh," she breathed, leading me down the hall. Then she swung open the door.

"We had a much better day yesterday," Nurse Frankson whispered as she took my mother's pulse. Then she fidgeted with her pillow. "She's had a lot of pain today and we've just given her an injection."

I stared at the nurse for a moment. Nurse Frankenstein would have been a better name. She was a good thirty centimetres taller than I was and she had a big, square head with a jaw you could crack nuts with. There was even a wart on her neck just above her collar. Now she was fixing my mother's sheet.

I wanted to scream, *Just leave her alone!*

"Don't stay too long, dear," she said before walking out the door.

"Hi, Mom," I whispered as I kissed my mother's

cheek. At last we were by ourselves. With her eyes closed, I wouldn't have recognized her. Plus there was this horrible sickly-sweet smell hanging around. It couldn't be Mom that smelled that way, could it?

But it was. The cancer that was eating her stank. Everything stank.

I rummaged frantically in my purse till I found a small sample bottle of cologne, "4711." It was a German cologne that Mom loved. Last Christmas she had put it in my stocking, while I had bought a larger bottle as my gift to her.

"I'll bring you your own tomorrow," I said as I dabbed some on her wrist and forehead. It made me feel good to do one small thing for her.

But it made me feel funny, too. My mother always used to put this same stuff on me—exactly like I was doing right now to her—when I was little, going to a birthday party or somewhere else special.

Now what could I do? I walked over to the window and looked out onto another hospital roof, its vents and metal chimney jagged against the sky. It wasn't a great view and to make it worse, a dead fly lay, tiny feet up, between the two panes of glass. DO NOT OPEN, warned a paper sign taped to the window frame.

I carried an armchair over to sit beside Mom. It hurt to look at her. I stared instead at the flecks in the linoleum tile.

Finally I raised my eyes—only to the level of her hand, where it rested near the edge of the bed. A plastic hospital bracelet circled her wrist. Her wrist bone stuck out large against the thinness of her arm.

A tube attached to a clear bag disappeared into skin that looked so fragile it might tear.

I looked up at her face.

Oh God, why does this have to happen to Mom? Why is this happening to me? I wanted to be far away—to be with Mark. I turned away for a moment.

No, I won't cry. I won't. Oh God. I had to close my eyes tightly for a few seconds. Then I turned back to her.

I saw the hollows in her cheeks and the purple shadows under her eyes. I tried to imagine Mom's face smiling again but I couldn't. Then all at once I knew I had to leave because I *was* going to cry.

"Mom, there was a lot of stuff I wanted to tell you about today." I stopped to listen to my own voice the way I once did when I called in to a disc jockey and didn't shut off the radio. My words echoed at me strangely. "Anyway, it doesn't really matter. I guess I can talk to you tomorrow when you're feeling better." If she ever did feel better.

My mother stirred a bit. I leaned over to kiss her goodbye. Then she said something I had to let sink in before I really understood it.

"Be a good girl," was what she said.

Now why did she say that? "Be a good girl." Imagine, those might be the last words she would ever say to me.

I'm always a good girl, I wanted to yell. *Where has it ever got me?*

But instead I spoke quietly. "I want more from you, Mom. Don't you dare die on me!" Then I walked away.

CHAPTER 7

"Pop, do you think you could at least put your empties away?" I said to my father when I got home. It was becoming harder to avoid Pop now that Mom wasn't around. I stuck a couple of fingers in two of the empty beer bottles in front of him.

"You don't give me a chance. I would have in a second."

"Sure, Pop," I said, not believing him and not hiding the fact.

"Yeah, as a matter of fact, I was just going in to check on supper. I would have done it at the same time."

"Supper? No kidding, you made supper?"

"Paprika chicken. What's the big deal? Come and have a look."

I dumped my books and my shopping bags in my room. The beer bottles still hooked on my fingers, I doubled back to the kitchen and released them into the case.

My father was looking in the oven. "Should be ready, Christina. What do you think?"

I bent over to check. The chicken looked pretty pasty. There were a few potatoes and whole carrots thrown in beside it. "Pop, I think you're supposed to sprinkle some paprika on it."

"You think? What do they teach you in home economics anyway?"

I got out some paprika and shook it over everything. Then I basted the chicken, threw on some more paprika, and shoved it back in the oven. "They teach me how to broil grapefruit, Pop. Remember, I never wanted to take home economics."

"Yeah, yeah. Broil grapefruit, huh? Good for you, you'll be able to cook for your fancy rich husband."

"I don't want to get married, Pop."

"No, Christa." He gave me his deep belly laugh. "You want to take technical drawing to meet all the boys, though." He rolled his eyes.

This was not really true but it was easier just to change the subject. "Where's Ron?" I asked as I set the table.

"Ronnie? He's over at Frank's house, hoping to get fed there. Hey, by the way, how come he's wearing my socks?"

"Because he has a hard time putting his dirty socks in the laundry hamper." I took the chicken out again and tried to fix some gravy. Then I served it up.

"If we keep eating like this, you're going to get even skinnier," my father said after a mouthful of chicken.

It was dry. The gravy was lumpy and the potatoes and carrots were tasteless.

"Tomorrow night, I'll broil us some grapefruit."

His belly shook again. "So how did it go with your mom? You saw her?"

"Awful. She was doped up and out of it."

"Too bad. She was looking forward to seeing you."

"Uh-huh." I tried to eat some of the awful supper we'd made.

"You know, I didn't care if you took technical drawing instead of home economics," Pop said after another few mouthfuls.

"So how come you made me take—"

"Mama wanted you to take home economics. It was Mama. She thought with her working she couldn't teach you things." He shrugged his shoulders. I chewed my chicken over this awhile.

"Me, I thought—you're a smart girl. You wanna cook something, you're gonna look at a book. Besides you're gonna be the prime minister. Whoever heard of a prime minister cooking for herself?"

Prime minister—what a laugh! That was back when I was six years old. Everyone else knew that I wanted to be a gym teacher. Pop had a lot of catching up to do.

Never mind.

With Ron out, at least he'd talked to me. And it made me feel good to know that he was on my side about home economics.

I would have to stop avoiding him. Maybe we could even become friends again.

After supper, I threw a load of laundry into the washing machine. By now the hamper had lots of Ron's socks in it. Ron and I would have to get closer, too.

I thought back to my mother's last words in the hospital. Was I being a good girl?

Now that I was in a better mood I knew Mom

probably hadn't meant anything special when she said that. It was just like tacking on "have a nice day" after you say goodbye to someone. Still, I hoped it wasn't her final goodbye.

I washed the dishes alone—missing my mother's company the most at this time of day. Then I put the wash into the dryer, went to my room, lay back on the bed, and read over my pattern instructions.

I wondered if I could finish the dress in time for the dance.

The dance. Could I even think of going? Especially now that I didn't even have Mark.

It was only four weeks away and projects took a long time to finish in home economics class. We alternated cooking and sewing days and there was always a line-up for the machines. We had to wait for the teacher to look over what we'd sewn and tell her the next step before we actually did it. I'd have to ask Mrs. Chang for permission to work on the dress at home if I wanted to have it ready for the dance. If I decided to go, that is.

Right now, that was a pretty big "if."

CHAPTER 8

The mornings were still awkward for me. Without the usual shouting or talking going on, the house was quiet in a funny kind of way. So that morning I switched on a rock station. I guess there were advantages to Pop leaving so early.

After plugging in the kettle and pouring out a bowl of cereal, I looked around for something to read. In the bathroom there was this month's copy of *Reader's Digest*. It would do, I thought, and picked it up.

The tea was steeping as I leafed through November's issue. I thought maybe I'd read the comedy columns to cheer myself up. Out of the corner of my eye I noticed Ron slinking off to the shower.

"There's some socks in the dryer for you," I said to my copy of the *Reader's Digest*, loud enough for the Phantom to hear. There was some muffled grumbling from the direction of the basement and I heard the dryer door *thunk* shut.

There, he'd heard me. I poured a tea and turned it into my usual hot lemonade. An article caught my eye as I continued flipping through the magazine. "Stress and Cancer," it was called.

Hmm. I skimmed through the blurbs about diet and "hereditary tendencies" to get to the latest medical findings about the causes of cancer.

There it was in print. We were the reason my mother was dying.

A chart showed how much stress different things caused—there were points for having a baby, moving, changing jobs, money problems, you name it. You were supposed to add them all up, and if the total points were more than a certain number, you were in danger of getting cancer. I figured that since my mother already had it, her total points must have been high.

There were all kinds of ways that we'd probably increased her stress score—my father's drinking and being laid off work so much, Ron and I fighting, Ron's swearing and arguing with her, my smart mouth, my mother slaving away over the sewing machines at Electro-Knit—and that was for us, too. All of these things added up to that big minus, cancer.

How could I have been angry at her for being sick? I should have been angry at me or Pop or Ron. I hated us all. The six-year-old in me that still believed in God hated Him too.

I flung the magazine away and at the same time accidentally knocked my teacup to the floor. It smashed.

Stupid, stupid. I snatched up the pieces. It was Mom's favourite cup, hand-painted with little blue-berries. Why did I always have to use that one?

I must have held onto the pieces too tightly. When I looked down, there was blood all over my hands. I had cut myself and I was glad.

Then later on I wasn't so glad about it. I had to bandage a few of my fingers and everyone asked a lot of dumb questions. It also made it next to impossible to pin my pattern pieces in home economics.

"Mrs. Chang, can I work on my dress at home?" I asked when she came around to inspect my work.

"Hmm." She paused to think it over. "Can your mother help you with it?"

I just couldn't blurt out that my mom was dying like I had done to Mrs. Petrovitch. I swallowed my heart back down to where it belonged and whispered, "Yes."

"Well then, if you finish pinning it and I can check that it's all done properly, you may cut it out at home." Or at the hospital, I thought, if I bring a pair of scissors with me. I slipped some into my purse. I stayed through most of my free period so I could finish pinning the pattern pieces to the fabric.

Before I left, Mrs. Chang came back from the staff room with her coffee.

"That's fine," she said, looking over my work. "Now don't forget to bring it back to class."

"I won't, Mrs. Chang. And thanks." Now maybe I'd be able to finish the dress in time for the dance. I dashed out of the room—to see Mark and Candy walking along the hall together. I was stuck behind them all the way to math class.

Why couldn't Mark look different to me now that he liked someone else? He still had those large ears that I loved and those big hands that could palm a basketball and make me feel tiny and feminine

42

when he held mine. I really wished I could feel differently towards him now, but I couldn't.

I wished, too, that it wasn't Candy he'd dumped me for. That kind of made me lose respect for him. I mean, she wasn't really beautiful, it was just that her body said "yes, yes, yes" before a guy even asked a question.

What about me? I wanted to shout at Mark. *I have hips and breasts too.* Mind you, maybe they look a little ridiculous on a Douglas fir.

Then I thought, just how superficial are you, Christina Dzuba—worrying about your gangly body when your mother is dying?

As the three of us walked into the classroom, Candy noticed me.

"Hi there, Chrissy. We were just talking about you."

Oh, great. At least they could leave me out of it!

"Mark was saying you might know how I could join cheerleaders."

I had to admit it. Candy would make the perfect cheerleader. "I think you just have to show up for practice," I said. "There might be one tonight, I'm not sure."

"Thanks!" She walked off towards her desk— although it's stretching things to call that movement of hers walking. *Wibbling*, would be more like it— half wiggling and half wobbling. You could even hear one pantyhosed thigh swish against the other. I was left in the embarrassing position of watching Mark watch her. Gross!

43

We went to our seats, and Mark leaned towards me. "Hey, Legs, did you get the answer to number five of the assignment?" He grinned, and I found I still loved that smile. I passed him my notebook and he winked at me.

So maybe I'd been dreaming when I thought that he liked me. Maybe he'd only been flirting with me all along. I had to tug at my notebook before he released it back into my hands. That must be it, I thought. He was only playing games with me the whole time.

I tried not to look his way any more.

In history, Old Cedar Chest gave back all the tests except mine. Maybe he'd lost it. I could still hope.

"Those of you who did not get their quiz answers back, please see me after class."

He made it sound as though there were others who had to stay behind. Of course, there weren't. When the class ended, I was the only one.

"Yes, Christina, about your test here...well, I really don't know what to say." He looked over his half-glasses at me. "Do you have any explanation?"

"I don't know what happened, sir. I just went blank."

He frowned and then twisted his mouth around for a while as he thought. "People do panic during exams, but you understand it's a habit you *will* have to conquer?" He paused to allow me to answer.

"Yes, sir."

"All right then. Please have one of your parents sign this." He handed me over my *Germany lost again*. "This will, unfortunately, give you a failing

44

grade for the term so far. Next time, do better!"

I had a tick in my throat that I was having trouble clearing and my purse was feeling extra heavy on my shoulder. There was Mom's bottle of "4711" and those home economics cutting shears in there. I shifted it and went on to the gym for practice.

What did I care that I was flunking history? There was still basketball. I was certainly doing well there. No one could take that away from me.

I was wrong as usual.

Big Mac blew his whistle and asked both the girls' and boys' teams to gather around him.

"Tomorrow," he began, "we'll be posting the final listing of the team. To those of you who aren't on it, we thank you for your efforts. Please come out and support the team anyway. To those of you who are, let me say it is a privilege to represent our school and we expect you to conduct yourselves accordingly. Just because you'll be leaving classes early for games, that doesn't allow you to miss assignments. We insist that your involvement in basketball not harm your academic standing. And I'm announcing a new rule. You must maintain at least a C-plus average and a passing grade in all your subjects to remain on the team. Thank you, good luck, and now—play ball."

Oh great. Why did he have to come up with this rule the day I started flunking a subject? Any other year my grades wouldn't have caused me any problems. Why did nothing good ever happen to me any more?

I worked hard during practice anyway. I'm going

to be the best player they ever kicked off the team, I told myself. And that helped. Every time the ball swooshed through the net, I felt I was winning some battle with someone. Although it wasn't the main battle.

Jennifer was as depressed as I was when we were changing back into street clothes.

"I'm going to be cut tomorrow. I know it," she said. "Maybe I should try out for cheerleading after all."

"Candy's going to try out for cheerleading too," I offered, knowing that this information wasn't going to help the situation.

"Oh, give me a break. Really?"

I raised my eyebrows and shrugged.

"Well, there goes that idea. I can't stand being around her." She slammed her locker shut. "Hey, what's wrong with you? Is it your mom...or something else?" She had just noticed how furiously I was brushing my hair.

"I flunked the history quiz."

"No. How badly? I mean if it's just a few points, you'll still have a passing grade."

"I got two out of a hundred."

"That bad, eh?"

I just nodded.

"You wanna join cheerleading too?"

I threw my hairbrush in her direction.

"Well, it was just a thought," she said and we both laughed.

"What am I going to do?" I said after we stopped.

"Look...you wanna stay on the team, right?"

46

"Sure. It's about the only fun I'm having right now."

"O.K. You're not gonna like this but...tell him what you're going through."

I started shaking my head.

"But you're not giving anyone a chance." She stopped talking and chewed the inside of her mouth. "No, eh? O.K. Just tell Cedar Chest you're having personal problems, whatever you wanna say. But get him to give you a make-up test. And this time, study for it."

"I don't know, Jen."

"Well, it's up to you but..." she crouched into a classic cheerleader pose and sprang up, shaking imaginary pompoms, "consider the alternatives."

CHAPTER 9

When I got to the hospital, there was no chanting going on and Mom was sitting up in bed. What a great surprise!

"Hey, Mom, you're feeling better!"

"Hi, Christina. I had the most wonderfool dream today." Mom still had an accent since she always spoke Slovak with the girls at work. "I dreamed I was eating blueberries picked fresh from the field, like when I was a girl—"

Like the ones on your favourite cup, I thought to myself.

"—and whipped cream, so much whipped cream on top, just like a little mountain. . . ."

"Do you think you could keep some whipped cream down?"

"I think maybe. . . ."

"I'll be right back."

I didn't bother with the elevator—it took too long. Instead I ran down the stairs, two at a time, to the cafeteria. There was a CLOSED sign across the window. I was breathing hard now and I felt panicky. Somehow I had to get her those blueberries and cream. Think, think, think!

There was a pastry store a few blocks from the

hospital. It was worth a try. I tore out of the hospital and dashed to the store.

The bell rang furiously as the door slammed behind me. "Please, sir...would you have any blueberries?" I said, panting.

The man looked at me with questions in his eyes.

"With whipped cream. It's for my mom. She's real sick and she thinks she could eat today...please."

"I have blueberry pie filling." He spoke slowly as if thinking it over.

"If you could just put some in a paper cup and spoon some whipped cream on top...would you have a plastic spoon?"

"Sure," he answered. Maybe he got lots of crazy requests. He looked softer as he rang up the sale. Eighty-nine cents, just as if it were an ordinary pastry.

"Oh great! Thanks." I almost threw my change at him.

"Good luck, young lady," he said. The kind of man who gives a firm handshake, Pop would say.

I had to slow down on the trip back, so I wouldn't spill any. Down the street, up the stairs, through the hall, back to Mom. I was gluing her favourite cup back together in my mind, trying desperately to make up for some of the stress points I had caused her.

When I went in her room, Mom had sunk deep into her pillow.

"Christa, is that you? Come closer." She was very groggy.

"Mom, I brought you blueberries, you know, like in your dream, with whipped cream."

"Hmm? What's that? Oh, Christa, I can't, I can't...."

"But you said—"

"Your mom's just had a shot," interrupted Nurse Frankenstein, marching into the room. "Why don't you eat her dessert for her, dear?" She gave me the kind of smile you give a little kid asking you about Santa Claus.

I set the paper cup down on the night table beside Mom's bed. Then I removed the large bottle of "4711" from my shoulder bag and placed it beside the blueberries and cream.

"I love you, Mom," I whispered near her cheek and then I kissed her goodbye.

CHAPTER 10

When I got home, I wasn't in the mood to cut the dress out. I dumped everything in my room and slumped down on the couch in the living room to watch TV.

My father came in from the kitchen with a plateful of macaroni dinner, hot dogs, and brown beans. That was in one hand. The other, of course, held a beer.

"Hey, look, I made our favourite," he said to me, ignoring my sneer. His belly shook a little at his own joke. "Here, you eat this, I'll get some more from the kitchen." He set the bottle down, too.

"Could you bring the ketchup, Pop?" I hollered after him. Now that food was in front of me, I was hungry. I ate quickly and then concentrated on the screen.

Just what I needed—a family show with good-looking parents and children. They lived in a house that looked as though it had just been redecorated and they laughed all the time. Why couldn't my life be more like that?

Next day, I decided I would do my best to make my family closer. I couldn't make them better-looking or richer, but I might be able to help us all get along better. After going to see Mom, I planned to visit the library and sign out a cookbook with a recipe for cabbage rolls in it. Then we'd have a real family dinner. If the cabbage rolls were good, maybe I could take some to Mom.

I'll tackle Old Cedar Chest today, too, I promised myself. I still didn't want to say anything about Mom to him. Maybe I wouldn't have to.

I finished my breakfast and quickly scrawled an imitation of my father's straight up and down signature on my history test—Paul Dzuba. I didn't feel guilty about it. There were just too many other things to feel bad about right then.

I packed up my books and left.

At school, Jennifer called to me as I approached my locker.

"Hi, Chris. Going to the gym at lunch?"

"Why? There's no practice today," I said opening my locker and flinging in my things.

"They're posting the names of those who made the team."

"Oh yeah, that's right." It was something that was more on Jennifer's mind than on mine. I knew my name was on—it was just keeping it on that was the problem. Poor Jen, she was chewing on her lips, hoping against hope to make the team.

"What's up with Wayne these days, anyway?" I asked, hoping to cheer her up.

"Well, he kind of winked at me in the hall the other day."

"Really? What do you mean 'kind of'?"

"He could've been winking at Candy. She was standing behind me at the time."

"Ah, must have been you. You're so much better looking than she is."

"Yeah, but you're forgetting I'm not enough of a 'real woman.'" Jennifer pushed out her chest in a Candy Thompson imitation. Giggling, we headed for class.

I had home economics first. That day, Mrs. Chang helped us make tea biscuits. They weren't as bad as the broiled grapefruit but they had a salty baking soda taste to them. Still, I made a note of the recipe. Maybe they'd go well with my cabbage rolls.

In history, I waited till everyone cleared the room before approaching Cedar Chest. He looked down through his funny black half-glasses at my test, now complete with my autograph.

"I wonder..." I began. He looked up at me. I won't be able to tell him if he keeps looking at me, I thought. I had to start again. "I was just wondering if maybe there was some way I could make up for my grade on the test."

"Well, well, Christina. Why the sudden concern?" He didn't wait for an answer. "Isn't it wonderful the effect of having your father sign the test?" He laughed, just like Pop would at some corny joke he had made.

I looked straight into his watery eyes.

He stopped laughing. "Yes, yes. I won't write a new test for you but you can do an essay—shall we say 2000 words—on the causes of World War II."

"Thank you, sir." I tried not to sound too relieved.

"Oh, and Christina." He left me hanging.

"Yes, sir?"

"Within the next two weeks please. Otherwise you won't be playing any basketball."

"Yes, sir."

Now how was I going to find time for that paper along with everything else?

When I got to the gym door, nobody was there. Jennifer must have rushed to the door the moment she got out of class. My name was the second on the list. Jennifer's was invisible.

Where would she have gone?

Entering the girls' locker room, I took a quick look around. Jennifer wasn't at her locker. I walked past the showers over to the bathrooms. There I recognized the navy pumps on a pair of legs that I could see between the stall door and the floor. I heard a few sniffles. Of course she was crying.

This was a crisis to Jennifer and I couldn't ignore it. Should I pretend not to know she was crying? Wasn't it stupid that really good friends wouldn't cry in front of each other?

I passed a kleenex underneath the stall. "Here, Jen. Don't use that toilet paper. Your nose'll get all red."

She mumbled, "Thanks." Then I heard a snort—blowing her nose or laughing at herself, I couldn't tell.

"That's O.K. Just return the favour when they post the names for the gymnastic team."

There, that was a snort of laughter. There was a flush and then the door swung open. Jennifer was trying to grin at me. I just shrugged my shoulders.

"Are you going to stay for the guys' game tonight?" I asked her.

"You?" she countered.

"Uh-huh. For all the good it's going to do me. I should go home and do some bust development exercises instead." Or work on my history essay, or sew my dress, or visit my mother, or vacuum the living room. A lot of things were squeezing in on me.

The rest of my classes went O.K. In math, I was actually starting to do well. It was like basketball. The X's and Y's were as controllable and predictable as the swoosh of the ball through the basket. It made me stop thinking about other things.

When Mark smiled my way, I couldn't stop myself from beaming back at him, but I answered coolly when he asked if I was going to watch his game.

"Yes, with a friend." I don't know why I said it in that way. I guess I wanted him to get the message that I was only doing it to keep Jennifer company.

But of course I wasn't.

When we got to the gym, Big Mac asked Jennifer and me if we would time and keep score of the game. Now this was a stroke of luck! We got to cut up the oranges at half-time and walk across the gym floor to serve them to the two teams.

We had to take all the names and shirt numbers down and then keep track of fouls and points scored. Jennifer did our Riverdale team and I did Jefferson High. One of the Jefferson guys sort of made a play for me as I took their names. I think it's one of their customs, to hit on a girl from the opposing school. He grinned and grabbed my hand. I just smiled and tugged it away.

Then the game started. Jen had the clock but she was helping me keep track of the other details, too.

"Foul on Number 10," she said.

"Ah, that's too bad. He's kind of cute." Number 10 was the hand-holding guy from Jefferson.

But it was Mark who made the foul shot. *Swoosh. Swoosh.* Right in the basket. Our cheerleaders leapt up, frantically waving their pompoms. Candy actually bounced higher than any of them.

The score was 2-0 for Riverdale. Back up the court, Mark was crashing through Number 10.

"Foul on Mark," Jennifer said. I ticked it off.

Back and forth. The score stayed really close, 26-24, then 38-32. Candy was able to work in some fancy moves. "Two, four, six, eight," she began to cheer. The others joined in. "Who do we appreciate? Yay, Mark!" He had made another basket.

"Ah, shut up," I muttered.

Jennifer chuckled in agreement.

Mark was also fouling a lot. The limit was five.

"Half-time," Jennifer said for my benefit and then blew timidly on her whistle. She was soon drowned out by the louder duet of the two referees.

We served the oranges. Jefferson's Number 10 wanted my phone number.

"I'm in the book. The only Dzuba in it." Of course the D was silent but I figured that if he was sharp enough to get the spelling right and went through the trouble of looking my name up, I might just go out with him. Maybe he could take me to the dance. After all, why should I stay home just because Mark took

Candy? If anything, I would go to the dance precisely because of them.

Jennifer wasn't doing well with Wayne. The guys from our team grabbed the oranges but ignored her. She didn't look pleased when she crossed back over the floor.

"Wayne's not going to ask me to the dance. He doesn't know I'm alive."

We both looked over in his direction. Our favourite pompom girl was over chatting with Mark and Wayne. Jennifer surprised me with how loud she blew her whistle.

Half-time was over.

Mark had the ball and was travelling up the court. Number 10 was checking him, too tightly I thought. Mark went up for a shot, bringing his knee up. Number 10 caught it in the stomach and crumpled. It always paid to exaggerate injuries to get the referee's attention. The referee called a double foul. Both players were charged.

I held up four fingers to the referee and then to Mark as a warning. One more, and he was out of the game. He looked like he was saying something unpleasant under his breath.

He flubbed his foul shot. More unpleasant words and then he took his place at the Riverdale court. He bent over waiting for a rebound. Number 10, however, made his. The score was now 48-44 for Riverdale.

Number 10 glued himself all over Mark as he brought the ball up the court. He was getting to

Mark. I saw them jostling in the corner. The referee didn't.

Number 10 snapped up the ball. Mark was losing his cool. He chased after him, two strides behind, right up until the time Number 10 jumped up to make his shot. Then Mark, in an act of desperation, slapped at him as he caught up, half a second too late.

The whistle shrieked. Candy suddenly woke up and started to cheer—for the wrong team.

"Oh, geez, I don't believe that girl," Jennifer said, grinning and shaking her head.

"Boy, aren't you glad you didn't try out for cheerleaders?"

"Shut up!" someone yelled at the cheerleaders and the cheer dissolved.

The referee whistled again, pointing to Mark and then imitating the illegal slapping motion he had made. The basket stood. I held up five fingers to the referee and then to Mark. My eyes were looking right into his. Then I made the hitchhiker hand signal to throw him out of the game.

That'll teach you to have lunch with Candy after holding hands with me, I thought. But after that quick wave of smugness passed over me, a sick feeling took its place. It occurred to me, at that moment, that I had just thumbed myself out of another chance with Mark.

We lost the game 52-48 and that put Riverdale at the bottom of the league.

"Poor Mark," Jennifer said to me. "You really should go over and comfort him."

"Very funny, Jen. Let the pompom queen do that. She even cheers him when he fouls out."

"I don't know, Chris. You should have seen the way he stared at you when you were serving the oranges to the Jefferson team."

"Really?"

"Really," Jennifer answered.

"I don't believe it," I said. But no matter what, I was going to finish that dress.

CHAPTER 11

I left the school and crossed the street on the way over to the hospital. Mark was at the bus stop on the other corner. With his duffle bag slung over one shoulder, his head hanging down, he was magnificent. In spite of everything, I wanted to run to him.

One large hand ran through his dark hair then passed quickly over his eyes.

I stopped myself.

He looked like he was crying. Now, I only know two other guys, my father and Ron—I mean, really well. They hate it if I catch them crying. So what could I do? Seeing him that way now, I realized that I hadn't thought of him as a real person. He was just a neat-looking guy who made me feel good when we hung around together. I knew then that if I took the time I would find that he was much more.

I thought I could forgive him for looking at Candy Thompson—although maybe not quite for having lunch with her. But I couldn't go to him right now.

So I just walked the other way.

It was the usual routine at the hospital. Frankenstein showed me into the room, hovering like some gigantic, annoying insect while she checked this, adjusted that, refilled the other—as though any of it made a difference.

"Not too long, eh, dear?" she said. They were the same words she left Mom's room with every day.

How could I possibly be too long?

I kissed my mother hello and then unfolded my material carefully on the empty bed next to her. I was afraid the rustly noise of the pinned pattern pieces might signal back Frankenstein. Doing anything out of the ordinary always seemed to be against some rule.

But no. Good.

The shears made a loud *whoot*, *whoot* noise as I cut through the jersey. Frankenstein must be deaf.

"I'm making this dress for my home economics class. Well, I'm really making it for the school dance," I said to Mom. This wasn't bad. When I didn't look at her, it wasn't so hard to talk. "I don't know. I think it will be for the dance. Anyway, I'm not sure I should go, with you being sick and everything. You remember Mark? Well, it looks like he likes this other girl now and won't ask me to go."

Whoot, *whoot*, the cutting shears answered.

"Jen didn't make the basketball team and she's really down. The guy she wants to go to the dance with just doesn't seem interested. Oh, and I flunked a history quiz. I was supposed to get you or Pop to sign it. Well, you weren't in any shape and Pop, you know how mad he gets sometimes, especially about bad grades. So I just signed it. Anyway, flunking the quiz was no big deal at first. I mean, next term I would have done better. But then the basketball coach announced a new rule about passing grades. So I threw myself on the history teacher's mercy and he's agreed to let me make up the test with an essay. Ten pages though.

"There's just so much to do all the time and I can't seem to get around to it all. I don't know how you used to do it, Mom. I wish you had told me how much work it was. I mean, making supper, doing laundry, and working, and everything. I wish I had helped you more. Do you think if I had, you wouldn't be sick now?"

I had finished cutting out the dress pieces by that time, and I looked at her.

She was mumbling something. I leaned over, my ear closer to her lips.

"Go, go," she said.

I straightened quickly, gathering up my things. She must be tired and wants me to leave, I thought. Her lips were still moving, so I leaned over again.

"Go without the boy. With Jenny, with Jenny. Go, go." I couldn't really understand her.

Halfway down on the elevator, what she said finally made sense. To the dance, that's what she meant. Go to the dance even if Mark doesn't ask me. She was giving me her blessing. Jennifer didn't have a guy to go with either. With the two of us going, we wouldn't feel so weird. I guess her telling me to go made it official. I would go.

Had I made her sick, though? She hadn't answered my real question. She hadn't told me what I really needed to know.

CHAPTER 12

Finally, it was Saturday. This was the day my mother always used to clean my room. I mean, I would vacuum the living room and maybe clean up the kitchen, but I hate my room and I managed to sneak off somewhere before it was straightened up.

It was designed to be a nursery and I *was* the baby—a long time ago.

Now it was just too small. Plus it was yellow, the shade that old pages turn into. Canada Hardware had a sale of Mastertone paint during the week I went camping with Jennifer, and her folks. Pop couldn't resist. He bought enough to even do my bookshelf, but not enough to do my bureau or my wobbly little desk. My flowered curtains and bedspread went perfectly with the colour my room used to be—blue. Now they fit just as perfectly into the overall effect of the room—barf.

But my mother loved it. When she was young, she had to share a room with her four brothers. So from her viewpoint, my room was a big step up. She even loved the colour. Maybe, come to think of it, she had something to do with it. The colour of sunshine, she would say.

She can be corny.

Anyway, now I was stuck with cleaning it myself. I

63

decided to begin with the bookshelf. In three movements of my arm, I swept the clutter off the shelves into a shopping bag. I had been ready to part with that junk a long time ago but Mom wasn't.

She would have dusted each momento of my childhood—the little dolls from Czechoslovakia, the blown glass deer, the stuffed lobster from a Maritime holiday—then placed them carefully back on the shelf. She liked her memories that way.

Next, I put the books strewn all over the floor back where they belonged. Then I hung up the clothes piled all over my chair, and opened the window.

That was one of my mother's tricks too, to air the room. She would also have hung the pillow and comforter out the window like she did with her feather beds in the "old country." So I gave my pillow a few shakes out the window. That's for you, Mom, I thought.

Then I quickly made up the bed and dust-mopped around and under it. Good enough, I thought, looking around.

I grabbed my guitar from the corner and gave it a few strums. G chord, F chord, C chord. That's about all I could play, but I liked the sound. It was relaxing. I picked the guitar up maybe once a month, so I didn't even have callouses on the tips of my fingers the way I used to.

Pop stuck his head around my door. "When are you going to see Mama today?"

"Later this afternoon, I guess. I want to go to the library first." We got in the habit of checking with each other. We were taking shifts with Mom now.

"Good, Ronnie's going around lunch. I'll see her now. You want to come grocery shopping around 4:00 then?"

"O.K., Pop."

"So bye." He closed the door.

I propped my guitar back up, collected a couple of pens and some loose-leaf and walked out the door. Stupid history paper.

As I left the house, the bus that drove by the library was rounding the corner.

I broke into my famous gazelle run. That's what Jennifer calls it when I really stretch my legs to get some speed up. It pays to have long legs sometimes.

I caught the bus.

It was only a short ride to the library. I sat at the front of the bus. I always do that so I don't have to ring the signal bell to get the driver to let me off.

There was the library, just ahead—I sprang out of my seat, held on to a bar as we lurched to a stop, then scrambled down the stairs.

Inside the library, the reference librarian pointed in the general direction of the history section. I found a whole shelf of books there, just on World War II. I removed a few fat volumes and thunked them on the table. Then I buried myself in one of them, scribbling down notes and checking my watch every fifteen minutes or so.

After a while I forgot to check, and suddenly it was 11:30. I had to leave.

I shelved the volumes and grabbed a smaller book

called *The Origins of the Second World War.*

I didn't remember the cookbook until I was standing in the check-out line.

I asked the librarian how to find a recipe for cabbage rolls and she keyboarded something into her computer. The answer came up *Russian Cooking* 641.5947. I walked over to that part of the library, found the book and then checked that out along with the history book.

Now, was there enough time to go home for some lunch? I glanced at my watch. No. Did I have enough money to grab a burger? I fingered the change in my pocket. Again no. Straight to the hospital then.

I used my change to ride the bus over, so I was there slightly ahead of schedule.

Ron was still in the room. I hesitated outside the door, wondering if I should go in. He was holding Mom's thin white hand, looking down at it, shaking his head. I heard him whispering and when his voice cracked at one point, I heard the word, *sorry*. That was all. Then he looked directly at her and I saw how that hurt him.

He kissed her gently, patted her hand, and then placed it back underneath the sheet. He walked towards the door.

"Hi," I said. He glanced at me and I saw that that cost him, too. But I didn't understand why. He went off without a word.

I went in to Mom.

Today I thought, I would talk to my mother about cooking. I flipped through my Russian cookbook.

There were pictures of coloured Easter Eggs all over it. The recipe they had in there for cabbage rolls said to wrap sour cabbage, (*sauerkraut* it said in brackets) around the rice and minced beef. That couldn't be the right one.

"Oh, Mom, I wish you could tell me how to make your cabbage rolls." She slept on, her breathing noisy like a light snore.

So I reread my history notes and began organizing them for the essay. The snoring continued. I leafed through *The Origins of the Second World War* and then began writing. It was great to stop worrying about the essay and actually do the thing. Nurse Frankenstein came back and began her checking routine.

It was too much for me, so I left.

When I got home, I made myself a cheese spread and ketchup sandwich and ate it as I checked the cupboards and fridge to make a grocery list.

Cereal, we were out of cereal. Bread, macaroni dinner, canned beans, minced beef was always good for hamburgers, spaghetti sauce. More laundry detergent, lemons, eggs—oh—and ice cream. I wouldn't want Ron to go without breakfast. Wieners, maybe some sandwich steaks, etc., etc.

Of course, when Pop and I actually got to the store and went up and down the aisles together, extra things ended up in the grocery cart. We both loved those chocolate-covered marshmallow cookies and we even opened the box and ate a row as we shopped. Mom wouldn't have allowed that. It amazed me that we were always on the same wavelength—at least when he wasn't drunk.

"You feel like some of Mama's cabbage rolls tonight?" Pop asked as we neared the check-out.

"Yeah, why, you know how to make them?" My father's squinty black eyes were laughing.

"Sure I know." He led me to the deli counter and, sitting between the potato salad and Bobo balls, were cabbage rolls. My father asked for some, and also some Bobo balls. "For Ronnie." He winked at me. "He doesn't like to eat ethnic."

So we ended up having my big "family" dinner. I even made my home economics tea biscuits and Ron wolfed down about six of them.

But it was quiet while we ate.

There was that empty chair. With everyone sitting around for once, that chair stuck out like a grave-stone.

Before I was anywhere near finished, Ron was scraping his chair across the floor and wiping his mouth with his shirt sleeve.

"I'll be at Frank's," he mumbled and then took off.

Did that ever bug me.

"You know you look so much like Mama," Pop said as if this was supposed to be telling me something about Ron's behaviour. "It's your eyes. They're that same funny colour that sometimes looks green and sometimes brown—and the expression around your mouth. That must be it." Then he shrugged his shoulders and finished the last tea biscuit. "It's good," he said.

I cleared the table. There were so many feelings my brother and I were sharing. Things I couldn't talk about to anyone else. If only we were closer. Why couldn't we be closer?

CHAPTER 13

The three weeks before the dance went by quickly. I finished up the history essay and got a B on it. There were basketball practices and games to go to, regular schoolwork to do, shopping and cleaning to keep up with at home. And my dress to get finished.

Every time we did sewing in home economics class, I would check with Mrs. Chang on the next pattern step. Then on Mom's old black machine at home, I would sew an extra seam or two in a push to get the outfit ready. For whom? I often wondered.

Mark sometimes looked as though he wanted to approach me and something was stopping him. I caught him watching me at times and I knew that he felt something still, but I wasn't sure what. Plus I still didn't know how I placed in terms of Candy, the "real woman."

"Jen, do you feel like going to the dance?" I asked as Jennifer and I did our end-of-the-day locker thing.

"Sure, but Wayne isn't going to ask me."

"Yeah, well neither is Mark. But I have my dress almost ready. And Mom even thought I should go."

"Alone?"

"Nah, dummy. We could go together."

"It's kind of a formal dance. Don't you think it would be strange?"

"I don't care. I think we should go."

Jennifer liked the idea. I could tell by the way she was pushing out her chin and chewing on the insides of her mouth. "Why not? You're probably a better dancer than Wayne anyways."

"Yeah, and I think you're way better-looking than Candy."

"O.K., Chris." She punched my shoulder. "That sounds good."

"Great, now I have a date for the dance." I turned away and walked straight into Mark. "Oh, sorry," I said and bent down to help him pick up his books.

He was trying to pick them up by himself and we accidently bumped heads.

"Ouch," he said.

"Sorry again," I handed him his books.

"It's O.K.," he said sadly as though he were pardoning me for killing his pet cat.

"I'm glad." I looked directly into his eyes, smiling, hoping for some response. His eyes were a field of grass, cool, green and inviting, but he didn't smile back. He walked away.

His reaction to our bumping into each other was so bizarre, it didn't even occur to me to wonder why he was up on my floor at this hour. I took the long walk over to the hospital, thinking about that look on his face.

Frankenstein greeted me by my mother's room. "Your mother tries so hard to stay awake for you when you come around. It's just that, as the day wears on, the pain gets too bad for her."

Just leave, I thought to myself and nodded as though I understood her. Fidget, adjust, fluff up. Finally, thank goodness, she left.

"Hi, Mom," I called out in my fake-happy voice. When I got to her bedside, it was difficult to be cheerful, no matter how well the rest of the day had gone. I kissed her warm face.

Today I was doing the hemming on the dress, the last step to its completion. I threaded the needle with far too long a thread. As I attempted to pull it through the material, I had to tug every now and again as the thread knotted and wouldn't go through.

It was slow, awkward work. The eighth time a knot formed, the thread snapped. I clicked my tongue, sat there thoroughly disgusted, and then began all over again with a shorter, more manageable thread.

Because the skirt part of the dress was A-line, the hemming job was a big one. I attempted a monologue with my mother. "I *am* going to the dance with Jennifer like you suggested. Neither of us really wanted to wait around till the last minute, hoping some guy would ask us. The dance is in a couple of nights, on Friday. I won't see you right after school but I'll come by just before the dance and show you the dress on me, O.K.?" I turned to her as though she might answer. It looked like her eyes were moving behind her lids.

"You know we had cabbage rolls the other night. Pop got them from the deli counter at the grocery store. It kind of made me feel good somehow to know you didn't make them from scratch. I guess there's a lot about you I really don't know." *And that I won't ever know.* I stopped for a second, trying to swallow down the rush of sadness.

"And I can't figure out why, but Ronnie won't talk to me. Won't talk to me—what am I saying—he won't look at me, won't walk to school with me, he can't even hang around the house if I'm around. I guess it's normal for a brother and sister our age to fight a lot or ignore each other. It's just that what's happening to both of us isn't normal and I think it would make it so much easier for me if I could talk to him. Talking about you with anyone else would just make them feel sorry for me."

My mother was breathing in shaky rattles.

"This hemming is ridiculous. I might as well leave the skirt here till tomorrow evening and finish it then. I have cooking in home economics at school tomorrow." I put the sewing stuff in her closet.

"So I'll see you then, Mom." I pressed my lips to her forehead.

Frankenstein waved goodbye to me as I passed her station.

When I got home, no one was there. I fixed myself a sandwich—some leftover Bobo balls cut in half, with hot mustard on a roll. It was really quite good. I took out some old photo albums and looked through them.

The first one had pictures of my mother when she was a girl. What another world she came from—with a kerchief around her hair and a long wide dress. She looked happy though, smiling not just with her mouth the way some people do for a picture, but with her eyes. Did she look like me?

I took out a later album with a picture of me in it. We did have the same eyes, although the skin crinkled around mine more like Pop's. Our hair was the same reddish-brown colour and had the same bumpy waves.

I looked at other pictures of her—some with my father, some on her wedding day (dressed in another ridiculous clown dress from that other era), some where she was holding first Ronnie, then me. She always looked so completely satisfied.

How was that possible? My father was always being laid off, or drinking, or both. My mother had to work so hard.

That's what I thought was so incredibly different about us. Our insides. I wasn't as good as she was. I always wanted more and better things—Scandinavian furniture for my room, clothes from *Young Teen* magazine. I wished my family was like the ones on television—a father with a college degree, dressed in a three-piece suit; a mother, healthy and at home, or at work on a real career. And a brother—well, right now I'd be happy if Ron were just not so angry all the time.

If my mother cared about these things, she never let on. I removed my favourite snapshot of her holding me when I was a baby. I was wearing one of those bunny-rabbit sleepers with ears on the hood. She was wearing a polka-dotted dress. We were looking into each other's eyes, smiling. My pudgy baby fingers were curled around two of hers.

Then at the last moment I took another picture out. It was me standing beside my father in the days when I was a lot shorter than him. I was holding a string with a tiny perch hanging from it, looking up at Pop, beaming. He had squished his old captain's hat down around my ears and he was smiling back—at me, not the camera.

I put both pictures in my wallet.

CHAPTER 14

It was the day before the dance. Jennifer and I made plans for me to go over to her house the next day after school, where we'd do our hair and make-up together. I still had over half of the skirt to hem but I'd stay up till my eyes bulged and my fingers bled to finish it in time.

"Jen, before the dance, you think your father could drop me off at the hospital? I promised my mother."

"Sure. I'll go in with you."

"Nah, you don't want to do that. I don't even know if my mother will know that I came or not."

"Look, it's all right. I'll go in with you. O.K.?"

"Sure. Thanks, Jen."

"No problem."

She didn't realize that it might be a problem. When she saw what my mother had become, she might not be in the mood for a dance. But there was no changing her mind. I could see her chin sticking out.

And maybe it was time for me to give someone a chance.

In Mrs. Chang's class we made chocolate chip oatmeal cookies. They were great! We weren't allowed to taste the batter, and when they were done, we could only eat three each. This for someone who could eat a whole row of chocolate marshmallow cookies in one sitting!

At lunch, I went to the gym and saw the names of the Basketball League's highest scorers. My name was third on the list. Spelled wrong as usual, but there nevertheless.

Someone was standing beside me as I checked over the names. Mark Hasting to be exact. His name was in second place. As I turned around, I was looking at his throat. His Adam's apple bobbed.

"Hi, how's it going?" I asked him.

"Not bad, I guess. You and I did all right on the chart."

C'mon smile, I willed. "Yeah, I do O.K. . . . in basketball," I answered, wishing he understood that I wanted us to go back to the way it was before he had lunch with Candy.

"You're going to the dance tomorrow night?" he asked, a half-smile passing across his mouth.

"Yeah," I answered, trying to keep my voice even. He's going to ask me, oh, please God, he's about to ask me, I know it.

"Well, maybe I'll see you there." Then he did smile, his uneven, white teeth turning the light on inside me again. I couldn't have been happier, except that—he didn't ask me!

The day wound down. Soon it was time to make my long walk to the hospital. I was tired and I knew that I had a lot of hemming to do. By the time I got to the nurses' station, I was depressed, as usual.

Frankenstein seemed excited as she greeted me.

She was holding something in her hand. It looked like black material. It was my skirt. Was this against some regulation, leaving a sewing project in a patient's room?

"Christina, your mother wore herself out trying to hem this skirt."

"My mother?"

"Yes, dear. She didn't want any medication and I could tell that her fingers were aching."

"I just left it here to work on tonight."

"Well, it seemed very important to your mother. So when she dozed off over it, I took it from her. The other nurses and I did a few stitches each till it was almost done. Then I put it back on your mom's bed."

"It's finished?"

"Yes. And your mom asked me if I could get it pressed. She wanted to make sure you'd look perfect for your dance." She handed me the skirt.

"Thanks a lot Nurse...Frankson." I hesitated. After thinking of her as Frankenstein for so long, it was hard to remember her real name. I felt like apologizing.

"There isn't much else we could do for her." She looked like she wanted to say something more but couldn't.

I went to my mother then.

"Hi, Mom. You know I could have finished the skirt myself. It was supposed to be my home economics project."

No answer as usual.

Suddenly, it was really important that she believe

me. "I mean, I was dreading doing it, but I could have done it. There's a lot of things that I'm doing now for myself."

As I stopped to look at her, I knew there was something I wanted to tell her, but I couldn't figure out how to say it. It was time for my mother to die.

She was trying to stay alive just to do things for me. The pain she went through to do that sewing, I didn't ever want her to have to feel again. I kissed her shrunken white hands and I kissed her face. I wanted to hug her, but I knew it would hurt her.

"Mom, thank you for doing that hemming." I cleared my throat. "I love you and I'm going to miss you. But I understand if you want to let go."

Still her breathing rattled on. Again I kissed her face. "Bye, Mom." I held up the skirt in front of me. "Tomorrow you'll see me wearing it." Then I folded it carefully over my arm and left.

CHAPTER 15

On my way to school the next day, I dropped off my dress and shoes at Jennifer's house. We walked the rest of the way together.

"You don't think it'll be weird going to the dance without a date?" Jennifer asked me.

"Nah, we can hang around the snack bar or, if we feel out of place, we can hide out in the bathroom."

Jennifer didn't say anything for a while. Then she asked, "Who do you think Candy is going with?"

"Hmm, good question. I thought with Mark. Why? You think she'll be there with Wayne?"

"Well, he's certainly done his share of gaping at her. She can't possibly go with both of them."

"You never can tell. Just one more reason for us to be there, isn't it? Mark is definitely going, I know that."

As we took our books out of our lockers, I thought I heard Jennifer say a strange thing. I thought she said, "Hope she goes with Wayne." But the bell rang and there was lots of other noise around so I could have heard wrong. I'd have to ask her what she meant, when I saw her later.

In the classroom, Candy was exchanging homework answers with Mark, smiling and gazing at him with those big, sad deer eyes of hers. Her hand was resting on his arm. *Touchy, touchy, feely, feely.* It was so easy for her to snare a guy.

Maybe I should stuff my bra with kleenex tonight. If I was going to be at the dance alone, I wanted to look devastating. I wanted to get lots of other guys to ask me to dance, or at least be a mysteriously beautiful figure at the snack bar.

At lunch, Jennifer was talking to some guy with glasses. I didn't know him. He looked a bit short for basketball but he was cute—in an egghead sort of way.

"See you later," I mouthed in her direction and waved.

It was late in the afternoon before I realized that I hadn't packed any jewellery to wear to the dance. Any other time, my mother and I would have gone through our jewellery together (a pretty pathetic collection even when combined), and picked something appropriate. Now it would have to be Jennifer and me.

After school, we went back to my house, and spread my mother's jewellery out on my bed.

Rhinestones were in big this year but neither Mom nor I had any. But there *was* that fancy garnet necklace of hers. My father had gotten it cheap from Bohemia, when a workie friend of his had smuggled it back after a trip to the "old country." I think she'd only worn it once or twice, to please him. But the colour was the same blood-red as the contrasting top panel of my dress. It would be perfect!

Next, Jennifer and I went through my jewellery box to find some earrings. I picked out some large gypsy hoops, since they were the only things that would show with my hair covering my ears the way it did. After I'd chosen, I shut the box quickly—but not quickly enough to avoid seeing Mom's wedding band. I opened the box up again and placed the ring on my finger.

What the heck, she might notice this evening.

Next we rushed over to Jennifer's house, to wash our hair. She had decided to curl the ends of hers, but I wasn't sure what to do with mine. Usually I just blow it dry, pulling it straight with the brush. Then Jennifer had a flash of brilliance.

"Why don't I put some mousse in your hair and make tiny braids all over? Then just before we leave, we'll take them out and it'll be all kinky. You know, the Vogue look."

"I like that. It'll be different."

It took forever, and in the end Jen only did the braids around my face.

Her mom made lasagna for supper. She knew it was my favourite. As we ate, I remembered our conversation at the locker.

"Hey Jen, what did you say this morning about Wayne taking Candy to the dance?"

"Huh? What did I say? I don't know. Let me take those braids out. We've got to get going if you want to stop at the hospital."

"You know, you said you hoped Wayne was taking Candy."

"They're still wet. I'll blow-dry them while you eat."

Maybe she had said she hoped Wayne *wasn't* taking Candy. Whatever, I thought. It really didn't matter. I shrugged my shoulders.

Out of the blue, Jennifer started talking about the Science Club she had joined after she had been cut from the basketball team. All excited, she prattled on about the kids in the club and the field trip they were planning. I didn't see how she got onto that topic, but that was O.K.

My hair was dry and she unwound the braids. It had turned into an absolute lion's mane but I liked it. I put on the garnets and a dab of "4711." We checked ourselves out in the dresser mirror.

"What do you think, Jen?" I snatched a handful of tissues from her box on the bureau and stuffed them into my bra.

"Big hair, big boobs. It's great. I love it."

Jennifer looked good, too. She was wearing a green slinky dress that contrasted with that great blond hair of hers. We were sophisticated. No one would dare say that we didn't look like "real women" tonight.

Her dad drove us to the hospital, where Nurse Frankson hurried us into my mother's room. "Your mother refused her shot tonight. She wanted to be awake to see you in your party clothes."

It was strange to see Mom sitting up in bed, her eyes open and sparkling with something that the cancer had still not been able to destroy. There was a tray in her lap full of the usual sickly hospital food— boiled this, stewed that.

"Mom, you're awake," I said, and went to sit on the edge of her bed.

"Hi, Mrs. Dzuba," Jennifer added formally.

"Girls, girls, you look wonderfool." She sounded really cheerful. Then something pulled across her face, a pain spasm, I suppose. She took my hand and I could tell she was trying to squeeze it. The effort was too much and she let go.

"Mom, we really can't stay long, we want to get to the dance by 7:15." She needed something for the pain and if we left, she would get it.

"No, no. Another moment." She put her hand on mine. It was as though a leaf had fallen on top of it.

Her face pulled together again.

"Mom, let me get the nurse, please."

"Just stay, my Christina." She smiled and I saw the same contentment on her face that showed in those old photographs.

Nurse Frankson scurried in behind us. "Mrs. Dzuba, please eat something before I take the tray away."

Then Mom looked at me and the ends of her mouth tugged first downward, then upward. She closed her eyes for one long second and then she looked at me again. "How can I? Nurse, just see." The leaf lifted off my hand and she gestured towards me. "I look at my daughter and I am full."

Jennifer slipped out of the room. I knew she was crying. I stayed while Nurse Frankson took out the tray and Mom got her shot. She kept smiling at me through it and I felt as though I was the centre of her universe. Then the tightness in her face relaxed and she drifted into sleep.

"Bye, Mom," I whispered. Then I hugged her, gently, gently. "I love you."

CHAPTER 16

I joined Jennifer outside in the hall.

Until then I hadn't cried, but when I saw her streaming eyes and red, running nose, well—the dam just broke. Jennifer put her arms around me and for a while we sobbed and sniffed in unison. It felt right. My best friend was sharing a bad time with me.

Then finally I broke away, removed some kleenex from each of my bra cups and handed one to Jennifer.

That made us both laugh.

"We better go to the bathroom and get rid of the Rudolph red-nose look," she said.

"Yeah, you're right. There's one just across the hall. Let's go."

"Chris," said Jennifer on the way into the bathroom, "I somehow never figured it was that bad. How do you keep everything going?"

Was I really keeping everything going? I looked at her. "I guess most of the time I'm just too busy to think about things much."

Then I went over to the sink and wrenched the cold water tap on full force.

Jennifer did the same and for a while we splashed our faces in silence. I blotted what was left of my mascara onto some more of my bra stuffing and put another layer of mascara on around my eyes.

"Now we have to go and have a good time," I said to Jennifer.

She nodded quietly, but I heard another few sniffs.

"No, really, Jen. Mom finished my dress for me. She was the one who insisted we go, even without dates."

"It's just that, up until now I never knew anyone who was dying before." She still looked really miserable, and there was nothing I could say. "And now," she went on, "it hits me that everyone I know will die."

"C'mon, let's go." Sure, everyone was going to die. It was something I'd been thinking a lot about myself lately, but I didn't want to go into it just then.

"Why should anyone bother running around doing all the things they do when everyone just dies?" Jennifer continued. We were dangerously close to another crying jag.

"Listen. Tonight we're alive and we're going to dance," I said. There was no other answer to give her.

We were pretty quiet on the drive over to the school, but our spirits were lifting a bit by the time we got there. It had been, after all, a good night with Mom. She had been awake, which was unusual. But more important was the contentment I saw on her face when she looked at me. I knew I had caused her pain sometimes, but I guess I had made her happy sometimes, too.

As we rolled into the parking lot, Jennifer's neck was craning to make out who was going into the school. The excitement of the dance was really getting to us.

"No Candy...there goes Mark."

One door slammed shut in my mind and another one opened. "Where, where?" I was stretching my neck, too.

"Too late. He went in already."

We slipped out of the car quickly and Jennifer's dad drove off. Then ahead of me I saw the swivel of familiar hips. Candy was wibbling her way up the steps with Wayne.

"Tough break, Jen." No answer. We went inside and headed for the snack bar. Jennifer smiled and waved at someone.

It was the egghead.

"There's Frank from my Science Club. You remember I told you about him?"

"No, Jen. I don't remember." Now she was grinning. Frank was walking towards us. "You dog," I said. "You must have told me just about everything else about the Science Club." That's why she didn't mind if Wayne took Candy to the dance!

She gave me a wicked chuckle. Then Frank joined us and Jennifer introduced him.

"Hi, Frank," I said. "Geez, will you guys just go ahead. I think I saw someone I have to talk to."

Jen mouthed a quick thank you over her shoulder as she and Frank took off in the direction of the dance floor. I gestured with my thumb to show my approval of her new partner. I guess I was going to be a lonely, beautiful, mysterious lady tonight.

But at the entrance to the gym, a familiar body was standing against the wall. The body was big and clumsy-looking, dressed in slightly formal, old-fashioned clothes. Mark's hands were in his pockets. He was alone.

I felt ridiculously happy.

This is the twentieth century, I thought, so I approached him. "Hi, Mark, music any good tonight?"

"Yeah, pretty good." He looked surprised to see me.

"You wanna dance then?" It felt great to stop waiting for him to come around.

He gave me this great big slow smile, then he took my hand and we went into the gym.

The music was perfect, slow enough for me to be in his arms and just sway. I thought I heard him humming. When it ended, neither of us noticed right away.

"Where's your date?" Mark asked me.

"Date?" I thought for a moment. "Oh, you must mean Jennifer! She's with this guy, Frank, from her Science Club."

"You mean you're not here with Peter?"

"Peter? Who's Peter?"

"Peter Jacobs from Jefferson High." I guess I still looked puzzled. "Number 10, the highest scorer of the League!"

"Why should I be with him?"

"I don't know. He kept talking about you during the basketball game, the girl with the great legs, he called you. He kept saying he was going to get your phone number. It got me so mad, I think I lost the whole game because of him."

"But I hardly spoke to him."

"Yeah, but when I finally went to ask you to the dance, I heard you say to Jennifer that you had a date." He stopped then, looking embarrassed that he had told me so much.

"Oh that! I was only kidding about having to go to the dance with her!"

"Ohhhh." The music started again. It was a faster song but we still ended up swaying in each other's arms.

"You look incredible tonight...so different!" he spoke softly, directly into my hair. His breath tickled against my ear.

"Thanks," I breathed into the side of his neck.

He held me tighter and it was like being swallowed up in his arms.

The next dance was too quick, so we went for a Coke. He never dropped my hand. I saw Jennifer at the snack bar with Frank and she just winked at me.

"Tell me something, Mark," I said, when we were off in the corner sipping our drinks. "Don't you like Candy?"

"Candy? Sure I like her." Then he hesitated. "Oh, you mean *like*, in the big way, the way I feel about you." Mark went red.

"Yeah."

"Nah, she's too short for me and too...fat. I like lean women."

"But I saw you having lunch with her and you were always walking around together."

"I always have lunch with Wayne, and Candy's his girl. You must have looked over when Wayne was still in line for his lunch or something." His uneven grin broke out. "Hey, Legs, you were jealous!"

"Of her? Not me!"

He looked straight at me with his great, green eyes.

"Well, sure I was jealous! What do you think!"

"C'mon then, let's take a walk."

We got our coats and walked out into what was now a cold night. When we got far enough from the school, he stopped, bent down, and kissed me. First I felt the quick brush of his lips against mine like the lick of a flame. Then his mouth lingered, gentle but insistent, and my own lips began to soften and part against his.

"You know," he said, pulling away, "I should have had that kiss about a month ago. Seems like I was gypped out of it a couple of times."

"Uh-huh," I said, still in a trance.

"If it had happened the way it was supposed to happen—I mean if you hadn't misunderstood about Candy and I hadn't misunderstood about Peter— we'd have had a lot more of this."

He kissed me again, slowly.

When we stopped, Mark removed his signet ring from his smallest finger. "So you don't feel jealous any more." He slipped it onto my middle finger, where it wouldn't fall off. "You should have been my girl a long time ago. I don't want to waste any more time."

Another ring.

I buried my face into his coat and cried.

"Hey, hey. What's the matter?" He pushed me away slightly and cupped my chin in his hands. His eyes looked directly into mine.

I wanted to tell him about Mom and about the wedding ring that I now wore. I wanted to share my sadness with someone who was important to me. I wanted to give the people I cared about a chance.

But at a school dance? When Mark had just given me his ring?

"Look, I really can't tell you right now. I...I'm going through something difficult. I'll tell you another time."

"Sure, Legs, sure." He took me back into his arms and kissed the top of my head.

No third degree from him. Yet without knowing it, he was giving me something I needed so badly. He was holding me.

CHAPTER 17

When I got home that night, Ron was waiting for me.

"I don't know how you can do that—go to a dance and make out with a guy while Mom's dying," he said.

"You've been spying on me," I countered.

He didn't answer.

"Mom wanted me to go. She hemmed my dress." He still said nothing. "I didn't make out with anyone." I was pleading with him. "I need to feel good sometimes. . . ." I noticed then that he was holding his head in his hands and his eyes were closed. I suddenly felt cold inside. "What do you mean, she's dying? Where's Pop?"

"At the hospital." My brother's voice was breaking. "Dr. Worden called. Mom's in a coma and he doesn't expect her to make it through the night." Ron covered his face with his hands.

"Let's go," I said softly and I went to call a cab.

At the hospital, Pop came out of the room to meet us. First he hugged us very hard and then I heard him swallow.

"You will listen to me now. Mama is going to die soon. But you are not to go in there and cry. We don't know if she can hear us or not, but you should tell her only happy things—speak of good memories—anything. Don't make her hold on to life because of your sadness. Let her go. Ronnie, first." Pop jerked his head towards the direction of Mom's room. Ron walked inside to see her.

Pop and I were alone.

"Come and sit down over here." Pop looked grey and his face was stubbly. "I'll go get us something from the machine."

I tried to think of what I would say to Mom. I had already told her I loved her, although I wished I could have shown it more. I had already told her that I could take care of myself, that she was free to leave this life. Oh, I hoped there was another life after this so we could meet again and so God could make this up to her.

Pop came back. I quickly ran my hands across my cheeks to wipe off the tears. I don't know how they got there. I was trying so hard.

"Look what I have here for you..." he said. He handed me some Coke, a bag of barbecue chips, and a box of Smarties. "Junk food," he continued, smiling, thinking himself clever to have remembered my favourite things.

"Smarties? Pop, honestly, how old do you think I am?" I lashed out at him.

He looked puzzled, lost for a moment. "When did you stop liking Smarties?" When did you grow up, was what he was really asking. Had he really not noticed the rift between us and the time continuing to pass?

I was sorry I had mentioned it. Why hurt him now when we were all hurting so bad anyway?

"Never mind, Pop. I still like them." I sipped at my drink and ripped open the bag of chips. I couldn't taste them. It was just something to do.

Ron came out of the room, his face drawn tight against his grief. He walked past Pop and me to the window at the end of the hall. There he stopped and stared out as if searching for something.

Pop patted my knee and softly said one word. "Go."

I gave him my chips, took one last sip of my drink and passed it over to him, too. Then I walked into the room.

There was a chair already near the head of the bed and I sat down quickly. Then I looked at her.

"Mom, I'm going to be O.K. I had fun at the dance. Mark liked my dress and he likes me. Did I tell you I was third highest scorer in the Basketball League? And I passed history."

I paused and reached into my purse for my wallet. "Here, look," I said, and I held out the snapshot of her with me as a baby in her arms. "My favourite picture in the family album. You and me."

Her eyes remained closed. Her breathing rattled louder and louder. It was the only sound in the room.

I wrapped my fingers around her hand much like I had done in the picture—only now my hand was the bigger one. I bit at my lip.

After a few moments, I let go and put the picture away again. I took the other one out and just stared at it. If only he would stop drinking, I thought. I put that one away, too.

"I know you love me." I twisted at her band on my finger. "I'll do my best to look after Pop and Ron... and I'll be a good girl...I love you, Mom." I put my hand on top of hers.

Then I got up out of the chair and walked to the window. Stupid, stupid fly, I thought as I stared at the dead bug where it still lay between the panes. Somebody must have had this window open for it to get trapped there in the first place, I thought. Quickly, I lifted the window up and snatched out the tiny body. I threw it in the basket and closed the window again.

And Mom stopped breathing. Just like that.

I ran into the corridor.

"Pop...she's gone." It was the bewildered voice of a six-year-old looking for her mother.

He stood up and held me tightly. "Ronnie!" he called out to my brother who was still standing frozen at the other end of the hall.

We all went into the room together. My mother looked relaxed, her mouth lifted slightly at the corners as though ready to break into a smile.

Pop said something to her in Slovak. Then he lifted her hand and kissed it. He turned to us.

"Goodbye, Mom. I love you." I kissed her cheek.

"Bye, Mom," Ron said in a whisper and then he kissed her too, lingering.

Pop put his hands on Ron's shoulder and drew him away. Then he kissed Mom one last time and lifted the sheet to cover her.

CHAPTER 18

On the third day we buried my mother. It was a brilliant white day. The sun was so bright it hurt my eyes. The air was frozen with the promise of the first snow. As the funeral drew to a close, we huddled together and the priest said a few words, first in Slovak then in English.

"Ashes to Ashes. Dust to Dust." He crossed himself and threw a handful of dirt on Mom's coffin.

My father, my brother, and I each placed a carnation on the coffin. We lingered a few extra moments and then left in a long black limousine.

Back at our house, people were all over the place—ancient, foreign-looking people. Women with leather skin, and babushkas tied around their heads; men in tired, baggy suits. My mother's cousin Maria had flown in from Buffalo and was serving everybody little sandwiches and sausages. Mrs. Petrovitch had brought a casserole full of cabbage rolls. Other food gifts had arrived over the past three days, and Maria had tucked them away in the refrigerator or freezer.

Ron had quickly holed himself up in his room, while the rest of the men separated themselves from the women and grouped around a vodka bottle. They were having an animated, bitter conversation. I heard a few words in English, something about "the tanks that rolled down the streets of Prague," and then the talk slipped back into Slovak. The speeches were punctuated every so often by a cry of "*Nostrovia*." The vodka would go down another several centimetres.

The women offered comments on how much I resembled Sonja, and how big, meaning tall, I was. To me directly, they said things like, "It was a blessing, a release." I knew that more than anyone—but somehow it didn't help right now.

Someone handed me a piece of cake on a small plate. "You must keep up your strength," the person said.

I took up my fork, dutifully, but as I dug the edge of it into the cake, I noticed the plate it was sitting on. It was the blueberry saucer that went with my mother's broken teacup. I placed the saucer with the cake back on the counter and exiled myself to my room.

I thought back to the funeral service. It had seemed a little less like an event occurring in another country. Nurse Frankson had been there, as well as Jennifer and her parents, our neighbors, Mr. MacDonald, and strangely enough—my home economics teacher, Mrs. Chang. In a quiet moment, she told me that her mother had also died of cancer, a couple of months before.

"When you're feeling less upset, I'd love to have someone to talk to, someone who's been through the same thing," she said to me. That would really be great, I thought. Maybe she could help me with the things I still couldn't understand.

Lying on my bed, I remembered the envelope I had pulled from our mailbox. From sheer habit, I had checked out the box when we arrived back from the cemetery. There had been no stamp on it—only my name, *Christina.* I had forgotten about it until now.

I sat up on my bed and opened it. It was one of those blank cards with a picture of the ocean at sunset on the front. On the inside, there were only two words: *Sorry*, and on the next line, *Mark.*

If only he could be with me now. He would look at me and I wouldn't hurt any more. No, maybe it was better that he wasn't there. Maybe I needed to feel out the sadness.

I changed out of my dress—it was the dance dress. I turned the skirt inside out and looked at the hemming. Then I touched it and felt a curious feeling of sadness mixed with, I guess, something that vaguely resembled happiness. Maybe it was the beginning of being close to my mother through good memories. The night of the dance had already become one of those.

In fact, the dance seemed like one of the happiest times of my life, compared to the last few days which had been so terrible. I fell asleep thinking that nothing would ever be as bad as this.

But I was wrong.

CHAPTER 19

As I drifted off, I still heard the occasional loud shout of "*Nostrovia*." They were solving the problems of the world, my father and his friends. Politics and vodka made them boisterous and loud.

Strange dreams invaded my sleep. There were people singing in powerful foreign voices and there was an open tank driving after my mother who was a young girl wearing my home economics dress. She got thinner and older as she ran. As I focussed in on the tank, I saw that it was my brother, my father, and I who were driving it.

"No, no!" I awoke moaning.

I didn't want to chance having that dream again so I dressed and went to the kitchen. I plugged in the kettle. My father was slumped over at the table, snoring.

There was never a more disgusting sight.

His face was dark with stubble and, when the teakettle screamed, I saw his baggy lids fold back to reveal red, glassy eyes.

"Christa, you are awake so soon?"

"You're drunk." It was time for the six-year-old to stop crying in the corner of the linen closet. I fixed myself a cup of tea.

"Ah, pour me a cup, too."

I glared at him as I handed him my cup.

"What is this ring you are wearing?"

"It's Mom's wedding band. You remember, you gave it to me." I deliberately misunderstood him.

"This ring." He put one of his square fingernails on top of Mark's signet ring.

"It was a present from Mark."

"At the age of fifteen," he smashed his fist down on the table, making my teacup jump, "you do not promise yourself to a boy."

"You stupid old drunk," I yelled, standing up. "In Canada, men give diamond rings when they want to marry you."

Pop liked us to speak our minds. "That's why we came to this country," he would say to Mom whenever she complained that Ron and I were "too fresh."

But this wasn't Pop. This was the stranger again. He shot up. His open hand crashed against my cheek. I lost my footing. He was breathing in and out like an agitated bull. I saw him in that moment, as the only driver in the tank which had run my mother down. I stood up again. "I hate you! You killed her with your stupid drinking."

He slapped me again.

Ron suddenly jumped in between us. Where had he come from? He pushed Pop backward, away from me. "Keep away from her, old man," he said in a menacing voice. My father swung at him. Ron ducked.

"C'mon, you stupid old drunk." Ron was needling him, challenging him, fists poised.

Why did Ron have to fight Pop? For me—finally he had to show feelings for me? I didn't want him to—not this way. Wasn't this all my fault? I had provoked Pop when he was drunk. Didn't I know better? My stinging cheeks didn't hurt half as much as seeing Ron and Pop fight.

There was so much love in that hospital room when we lost Mom. Now where had it gone? This fighting was worse than death. We all hated each other now.

I couldn't watch. I ran out the door without even grabbing a coat. I ran and ran and ran. I couldn't stop running. But where could I go? Who was there left to turn to?

I found myself shivering and panting on the concrete steps in front of Jennifer's house. I pounded on the door. Her mother, dressed in her robe, opened it.

"Why, Christina, you have no coat on—come in, you'll catch your—" She caught herself before completing the phrase. Her eyes took in the finger marks across my face.

Jennifer was still in her pyjamas, eating a bowl of cereal. Her mouth dropped open when she saw me walk into the kitchen. Her mother hugged me and I started hiccup-crying.

"Sit down, dear." She guided me to a chair. "I'll fix you a cup of hot chocolate."

What could I possibly say to explain to them what was happening at our house? How could I talk about Ron fighting Pop to defend me? What kind of monster did that make Pop out to be? If I told them about the stranger, the other person Pop became when he was drinking, wasn't it disloyal to the real Pop? Wouldn't I lose him then?

I said nothing—I couldn't—and surprisingly enough they accepted that.

Jennifer's mother remained quiet for a while. "Why don't you stay over a few days?" she suggested at last. "I'll phone your dad and let him know where you are." She had thrown me a life line. Right at that point I didn't think I could ever go back home. I nodded quickly.

Only for a few days, I thought. Sooner or later I would have to face them again. But at least not now.

CHAPTER 20

That day, Jennifer's mom made us stay home from school. She rented some movies for us and made popcorn.

It was a great idea. I didn't have to talk. The room was dark. I could let the occasional tear slip down my cheek and no one would notice. Every now and again, what had happened that morning replayed inside my head, but then the movies took those scenes away. I even fell asleep near the end of the second one.

The next day, we went to school. I borrowed something of Jennifer's to wear. I wasn't ready to face a lot of people yet, but it seemed everyone avoided me, anyway.

Except Mark. He found me sitting on a bench in the gym, twirling a basketball in my hands.

He sat down beside me. "You O.K., Christina?"

"No. I won't ever be O.K. again."

"Shhh." He pulled me into his arms. I stayed there for what felt like a long, long time.

"It isn't just Mom dying," I said finally. "It's that she was the whole family. Without her—well—my dad's just gonna drink. He and Ron even had a fist fight yesterday. I can't see how anything will ever get better." How could it ever get better?

"Things only get so bad, Legs, then they have to get better." Mark kissed my hand. Then he held me some more and stroked my hair.

Just as Mark got up to go, Ron walked into the gym. If I were in a normal mood I would have laughed out loud at him. He was dressed in the most bizarre shade of pink.

"I did the laundry last night," Ron said with a smile when he noticed me looking at his pants. "Do you own a pair of red socks?" We both laughed.

Suddenly, Ron looked at me solemnly. "Look, what happened between me and Pop yesterday was no big deal. Really. It's happened before when he's been drinking. You don't have to feel bad about it. . . ." He paused. "I won't let him touch you again and that's a promise."

The scene was replaying in my mind.

"Anyway, Pop said he would never hit you again, either."

Pop said . . . . Click. The scene stopped.

"When I went into Mom's room that last time, I told her what I thought she'd most want to hear—that I would look after you and Pop," Ron continued.

"Isn't that funny," I said with a short, dry laugh.

"What is?" he asked.

"That's what I promised her, too."

Ron gave a sad, resigned shake of his head. His eyes squeezed shut for a moment and then he looked away.

"Why do you have to do that?" I asked. I could hear my voice breaking.

"Do what?" He still wasn't looking at me.

"You looked away from me. Why can't you look at me?" His eyes met mine then. He closed them again and covered his face with his hands.

"It's just that I don't see *you* any more," he sobbed. "When I look at you, I see Mom."

I didn't know what to say. I just put my arms around him and cried too. Would it ever stop hurting? When I let go of him, he looked at me again. "I think after a while, I'll probably be glad to be reminded of her." I just nodded. We were quiet for a moment.

"Sooo...." he broke the silence. "When are you gonna come home, maybe give me some pointers about sorting laundry?"

"Soon," I said, knowing that I wasn't ready just yet.

CHAPTER 21

"Do you think stress causes cancer?" I asked Mrs. Chang after the others left the class the next day.

"Well, I suppose worrying is never good for one's health." She was looking me over to see the real intent of my question.

"But if a person had a real hard life, lots of money problems and things, could that bring it on?"

"My mother had everything she could ever want, a family, lots of money, maids to help out. She still died of cancer."

"Yeah, but was her family, I mean, did everyone fight all the time? Was she happy?"

"I truly believe she was, but, yes, my brothers and I fought all the time."

But I bet no one had a drinking problem. I was thinking though, as she was saying this, how contented my mother looked in the photo album. Was my mother happy?

Mrs. Chang interrupted my thoughts. "Have you seen this picture of my little girl?"

What I saw in the photo was a regular baby—cute but typical. But Mrs. Chang was gazing at the picture as if she were under a spell. That baby could have been a full moon on a clear night.

I was reminded of the snapshots that I carried

around in my wallet, the ones where both Mom and Pop were looking at me that same goofy way.

"I lose a lot of sleep with May's colic. But I don't think anyone has ever brought me more happiness. I'm sorry, but does that answer your question at all?"

"Yes, I think so."

"Good, good," she murmured and we walked out the door together.

In a way, she had answered my question. But I needed to talk to one more person.

My father showed up at noon, holding up his lunch pail, pointing to it and then to me, to ask in sign language whether I would go for lunch with him. This time I didn't even care if anyone saw us.

I nodded and as I got closer he threw an arm around my shoulder. He had to stretch it up to do this. That was the way we walked to the car.

We drove to the cemetery and walked up to my mother's grave, a pitiful, brown mound with decaying flowers strewn over it. Flakes of snow were beginning to drift down from the sky.

"Why are we here, Pop?"

"Because, Christa, before God and your mother, I want to swear that I will never hit you again." His voice shook as he said it. "I would have never done it if I wasn't drinking, so. . .no more drink."

"C'mon, Pop," I said in an unbelieving tone.

"You think I killed your mother with it?" I couldn't answer him. "I thought that, too, so I drank even more to forget. Then I hit you. Such a thing, Christa. No more, I swear."

Well, then I did believe him, and I told him so. We went to our other park to have mock chicken on kaiser buns and tea with lemon, the way I like it. It was strange to have an outdoor picnic in what was developing into a heavy snowfall. There were some extra bread slices to feed the birds and we did that, too.

"Christa, while we are here talking, my smart girl, when did I ever sign your history test?" How did he find out? "And with such an ugly handwriting. When your teacher showed this to me, I said to myself, Paul, you must have been drunk when you did this." He winked at me. "He says—all the other teachers say, too—that you are doing O.K. You *are* doing O.K., Christa?"

"Yes, Pop." As I said it, I was beginning to believe it, too.

"Do you know I met Mama when she was fifteen?" He picked up my hand and held on to the wedding ring. "This I gave her when she was seventeen. This ring," he switched to my other hand, to the ring Mark had given me, "does it mean you have changed your mind about marrying?"

I shrugged my shoulders.

"Is good. You will be the first married woman prime minister of...."

"Gym teacher," I interrupted. It was time for Pop to catch up with the fifteen-year-old Christina Dzuba.

"Gym teacher?" he repeated. "But don't gym teachers get married all the time in Canada?" Pop winked. Then his belly shook at his dumb joke.

And as dumb as the joke was, I laughed too.

109

ABOUT THE AUTHOR

Sylvia McNicoll graduated from Concordia University with a B.A. Specialization in English. She now resides with her husband and three children in Burlington, Ontario where she enjoys writing for young people of all ages and reading levels. *Blueberries and Whipped Cream*, her first novel, was originally written as a project for a children's writing course given by Paul Kropp.

Other books in the Jeanpac Series you might want to read:

Into That Darkness Peering
  by Grace Richardson

The Stone in the Meadow
  by Karleen Bradford

The Other Elizabeth
  by Karleen Bradford

Skate Like the Wind
  by Joan Ford